Bounty by Chance

Jeremiah Hackett is a young man searching for a future. On his quest, he teams up with huckster George Finimin, a tonic salesman. When Finimin is murdered, Jeremiah dedicates himself to finding the killer.

But things do not prove straightforward for Jeremiah, and he needs to mature and learn some harsh lessons before he can finally achieve his aim.

Bounty by Chance

J.L. Guin

A Black Horse Western

ROBERT HALE

© J.L. Guin 2018
First published in Great Britain 2018

ISBN 978-0-7198-2722-8

The Crowood Press
The Stable Block
Crowood Lane
Ramsbury
Marlborough
Wiltshire SN8 2HR

www.bhwesterns.com

Robert Hale is an imprint
of The Crowood Press

Typeset by
Derek Doyle & Associates, Shaw Heath
Printed and bound in Great Britain by
CPI Group (UK) Ltd, Croydon, CR0 4YY

CHAPTER 1

Southeastern Arkansas, 1878

Darkness surrounded the small campfire where middle-aged George Finimin and his much younger assistant, Jeremiah Hackett sat while having their after-supper cup of coffee. George and Jeremiah were roving tonic sales-men. For the past three years, the pair had traveled around selling products at any opportunity. In the fall, with no defined route, they would travel as far north as Independence and St Joseph then work the smaller towns eastward to St Louis where Finimin would replenish his inventory from jobber warehouses. Finimin and Jeremiah would spend a week at the Grand Hotel before migrating south to beat the cold winters.

They worked well together and considered themselves friends.

George and Jeremiah, with no particular route in mind, had traveled deep into the South, hawking various potions. One evening, near a small town in the southern part of Arkansas, an incident occurred that forever changed each of the peddlers in a different way. The men were camped on the banks of the Ouachita River near the small town of Arkadelphia.

The glow of the campfire provided the only immediate

light to the area as cloud cover hid the moon. The two were strangers to this part of the country and did not intend on a lengthy stay. They had canvassed the surrounding farms for two days, making a few small sales, and were making plans on striking out for new territory at first light; perhaps back to a more familiar area.

A hushed silence came upon the camp, when four men stepped out of the darkness to surround the two men seated before the flickering campfire. George Finimin, dressed in broadcloth, stood to address the visitors. One of the intruders, the apparent leader of the group held a shotgun across his middle in a menacing manner. Two of the intruders were large in body and young, eighteen or so. They wore scruffy-looking work clothes, brogan lace-up work boots and grease-stained floppy-brimmed hats. Each had an old cap and ball Walker Colt six-gun stuck in a holster belted at the waist and held sour expressions on sun scared faces, standing there with balled fists at their sides. The other two men were older. Emil Croft, the father of the younger men, held a twelve-gauge shotgun pointed menacingly toward Finimin. Harold Menning, Croft's brother-in-law, stood nearby, hands at his side and appeared unarmed. Finimin set aside the coffee cup in his hand and stood to face the shotgun-wielding man, who was red in the face and appeared highly agitated.

Finimin, concerned of the intrusion, perhaps frightened, recognized Croft from the visit he and Jeremiah had made to the Menning farm the day before. 'Gentlemen, we have plenty of coffee in our humble little camp,' Finimin offered.

When he received no reply, George then asked, 'Can I be of assistance to you in some way?'

The shotgun-wielding man, Emil Croft, spat to his side then said, 'Yesterday you sold me a bottle of some miracle mixture; some cure you claimed would ease my wife's pain and make her feel better. Later on, I noticed that she had drank the damn stuff and it killed her! She went to sleep, bless her soul, and never woke up. We are here to ask a few questions and exact some retribution.'

George had given the bed-ridden, almost comatose woman a spoonful of Laudanum (a solution of opium and alcohol) to ease her pains. He left a half-pint bottle with her. One spoonful every six hours were the directions for dosage printed on the label. Apparently, in a delirium, the woman woke up and drank the entire contents of the bottle! The deceased in question would most likely have succumbed to the prolonged effects of a mysterious fever anyway, but such a large dose of the powerful narcotic was too much for the woman's troubled system, resulting in her expiration.

George, flabbergasted by the news, nevertheless sought to defuse the confrontation. He held his hand out, palm down, in a calming manner.

'I am truly sorry to hear of the loss of your loved one, sir. Only the Lord knows when our time is due. I can assure you that in no way the bottled goods I sold would give cause for calamity. The ingredients are quite safe when taken as directed and, if you will remember, I was quite specific about that.'

The man holding the shotgun remained silent. George turned to Harold Menning, in hope that the quiet and subdued man would intervene. 'What I sold to your friend was Laudanum, a mixture that is recommended and used by almost all doctors as a pain reliever,' he pleaded.

Menning did not reply.

'Show me proof of your medical credentials, mister!'

the distraught husband of the deceased woman demanded.

George held out his hand. 'Please, sir, hear me out, I am not a licensed doctor,' he pleaded.

Croft shook his head from side to side when George continued, 'Your poor wife was too far gone for those in the medical field to save her, but I can assure you....'

'The only thing you are assured of, mister, is a place in hell,' Croft cut in. 'Why, you're nothing but a poison seller. Just as bad as a thief in the night, and hoping to be gone with the money you extracted before you have to answer for your foul deeds. Well, no more,' he scowled.

Finimin held his hands, palms out, at chest level in an attempt to calm and further explain. Croft, unsatisfied with Finimin's answers made a motion with the barrel of the weapon, which was apparently a signal to his youngest son who had been standing in the darkness outside the campfire's glow. Finimin continued his attempts to reason with the irate man holding the shotgun when the younger man stepped forward and swung a vicious blow to Finimin's head.

The brutal hit knocked Finimin to the ground and ended any further pleas of reason. The attacker followed up by standing over his target to rain fist after fist to the stunned man's face, which rendered the downed Finimin to unconsciousness. The other young intruder attacked the still-seated Jeremiah in a like manner. Jeremiah, stunned by the blows, tried to roll away and attempted to put his hands out in an effort to fend off the slashing fists that kept raining down on his face. After one well-placed vicious blow to the head that made bright lights flash before Jeremiah's eyes, his hands fell to his side as darkness took over. The aggressor must have figured that Jeremiah was done for because the attack stopped.

Jeremiah, helpless to do anything but lie still, appeared to be out but he was conscious enough to hear what was going on around him.

'That's enough, Judson,' Croft said to the brutal young man to get him to stop pounding on Finimin. The attacker swung one more clubbing blow to the downed man then backed away with his fists still balled.

Emil Croft, his face flushed with rage, stepped to stand over George, who was lying on his back unconscious. 'You lying son-of-a-bitch, you will bring no more misery to anyone ever again.' As if following a script, he pointed the muzzle of the gun to the inert George's middle and pulled the trigger, causing George's body to bounce from the impact. The twelve-gauge blast echoed in the still night, and the rotten egg odor of burned black powder hung in a cloud. George's body twitched in reaction from the elimination of his stomach, spleen and kidneys, but there was no longer life left in the man. The man holding the shotgun glared evilly at the body of the man he had just killed, while cordite and smoke from the fired shell rose in the air.

Jeremiah heard one of the older men say, 'Judson, go help Clarence take care of the carriage while we finish up here.'

The next thing Jeremiah heard was a loud crash and bottles breaking as the two young thugs turned the carriage over on its side. Unable to move his arms and with his brain still foggy from the beating, Jeremiah managed to open his eyes to a slit. From his position on the ground, he was facing toward the carriage. He watched as the two young men ransacked the its contents.

Then both men left the trashing of the carriage and rushed to stand over George's lifeless body. They each pulled their Walker Colts from their middle and fired a useless round into the dead man. The shooters would have most likely disposed of Jeremiah as well if not for the intervention of Harold Menning. Croft had turned his weapon to point toward Jeremiah, who lay a few feet away while the younger men, with six-guns in hand, waited for their father's lead. But Harold Menning quickly stepped forward to put a hand to Emil Croft's shoulder. Croft shook Menning's hand away, but his brother-in-law was insistent, stepping between the irate man and Jeremiah.

'Emil, that's enough, "an eye for an eye" so says the book. There is no need to damn your soul by bringing harm to another. He's just a kid. You have avenged Maggie's death by smiting the killer. We should allow this one to go back and spread the word, to his kind, to stop their blasphemy for money,' he instructed.

Clarence Croft stepped forward with his six-gun in hand, 'I say we kill him too! He's just as guilty as the other one.'

Menning held up a hand. 'No, no, Clarence,' he pleaded. 'That boy merely sat in the carriage the whole time the other one was in the house.' He turned to face Emil and said emphatically, 'No, Emil.'

After a few moments of silence, Croft nodded then said, 'So be it.' Clarence was not happy with his father's decision and exhibited it by slamming his six-gun into his homemade holster. He and the others then turned silently and walked away, apparently feeling their actions were justified.

Jeremiah, hurting from the beating, was only semi-conscious, his eyes almost swollen shut. He was horrified at having witnessed the cold-blooded murder of George Finimin.

CHAPTER 2

Three years earlier, in a different State further north, George Finimin and Jeremiah Hackett had come to know one another by chance. At that time, if anyone were to describe Jeremiah, most would take a quick look at the seventeen-year-old and say he was just a tall gangling kid. Jeremiah was that for sure. His five feet ten-height and one hundred forty-pounds weight gave the appearance of a harsh if not sickly appearance. He had a hawkish face and piercing ice blue eyes accented by a mop of collar length blonde hair. His clothing, though clean, consisted of faded patched jeans, a homespun shirt, run-down brogan shoes and a floppy hat that appeared to have been salvaged from someone's throw away.

Jeremiah was born and raised in the southeast corner of Arkansas. The rich loamy soil produced some of the largest watermelons in the south; the money received for the green-skinned melons, known for their sweetness, was a bonus to his family when sold. His impoverished parents sharecropped a small farm, planting crops of cotton and or black-eyed peas to satisfy the landowner's requirement as rent for the place. The landowner let them keep any moneys made from the sale of the melons.

At age ten, when both of Jeremiah's parents succumbed to a fever, the authorities delivered him to nearby relatives to finish his rearing. He had learned quickly that there were those, namely his uncle Charles, who would work him daylight to dark for nothing more than food as payment.

Uncle Charles resented being stuck raising his sister's offspring. For the first couple of years, Charles merely tolerated Jeremiah, paying little attention to the lad, and leaving his care and raising to his wife Matilda. Things began to change when Jeremiah turned twelve. Each morning at the breakfast table, Uncle Charles would assign jobs to Jeremiah. After supper, Charles would demand an accounting of what Jeremiah had accomplished that day. If Charles did not think the jobs given Jeremiah were to his satisfaction, he would say so and would not hesitate to give the youth a few swipes with a leather belt to ensure that Jeremiah understood. Although Aunt Matilda at times would intervene, Uncle Charles's wrath toward Jeremiah grew more aggressive for what seemed like the slightest provocation. By the time Jeremiah turned fifteen, Uncle Charles no longer picked up the belt. The man switched to using his fists to punish. Jeremiah tried his best to do exactly as told but it seemed that no matter what, he could not satisfy his Uncle's demands. One Saturday, when Charles and Matilda were away in town, a skinny stray dog, with his ribs showing, came into the yard. Jeremiah felt sorry for the animal and gave the starved animal some leftovers from last night's supper.

When Aunt Matilda and Uncle Charles came home and saw the dog lying nearby, Charles frowned in fury, 'Why the hell did you feed that worthless cur our good food, Jeremiah? For that, you get no supper tonight, but first I'm going to have to teach you another lesson.'

He quick-stepped to face Jeremiah, and then swung a fist to the side of his head. Two additional hard punches to the jaw put Jeremiah out. Later, he awoke to find Aunt Matilda swabbing his face with a cool wet cloth.

'It's OK, Jeremiah, he'll get over it,' she cooed.

As he lay there in misery, it became clear to Jeremiah that it was time for him to strike out on his own.

Jeremiah left his Uncle Charles' farm in the middle of that night, taking nothing with him but a folding pocketknife and a small bundle of food left over from the evening meal. He wandered aimlessly for a time and was welcomed at distant farms. The owners took pity on the youth, allowing him to do a little work in exchange for meals. Eventually his travels on foot took him north to Joplin, Missouri. He found out quickly that with no skills to offer he could only sustain himself by doing any chore that business owners would offer for food or payment. Most of these were the cleaning of horse stalls, shining boots, cleaning spittoons or running messages for anyone offering a nickel or dime.

Almost a year after he had left Uncle Charles' farm, Jeremiah made the acquaintance of traveling huckster George Finimin, who made his living by selling bottled concoctions claiming to cure all aches, pains and illnesses. Finimin had come to town to hawk his wares and often hired a down-on-their-luck local, usually a kid or a town drunk, to handle mundane chores for pennies. Finimin could recognize a downtrodden person easy enough and took full advantage, having the hired hand care for his mule, grease the carriage axles even wash last night's dirty dishes. He would point out various chores for Jeremiah to do, then excuse himself to concentrate on his inventory of bottled goods.

Finimin traveled around the country in a light delivery, one-horsedrawn black box carriage, which had the appearance of an undertaker's vehicle. The carriage was the perfect vehicle for Finimin and the lightweight wares within, which he promoted and sold to anyone with the cash. He advertised his business with six-inch white letters painted on both sides of the black carriage: 'Elixirs, Potions, Tonics.' Those three words settled any questions of what was inside. Underneath this, in smaller, one-inch high letters, 'Dr Finimin's Golden Elixir' was written in yellow paint.

When Jeremiah stepped to take a closer look at Finimin's little mule, Chelsea, Finimin drew him into conversation, seeming to take a shine to the lanky youngster, then offered food and a little pay if Jeremiah would take care of some things that he needed done. With no other offers readily available, Jeremiah did as Finimin directed for the next three days. The two talked at night, Jeremiah disclosing his reason for wandering. When it was time for Finimin to leave, the man, perhaps with a bit of sympathy for the youth's homeless plight, suggested that Jeremiah travel with him. He offered food and possibly some money payment later in exchange for Jeremiah taking care of the daily camp chores and caring for Chelsea, Finimin's little hinny mare, the offspring of a stallion horse and a jenny donkey. Chelsea was smaller in stature than the larger mules produced by the mating of a male donkey and a female horse. Jeremiah agreed to Finimin's proposal, then he and Finimin left town.

After a few days of travel, Finimin grew to like the hard-working young man, who would set to work setting up a camp as soon as the day's travel was finished. Jeremiah would cook what was available, often snaring a rabbit to add to their larder, then clean up after each meal and give great care to Chelsea. Finimin, for whatever reason, perhaps in greed or laziness, decided to take advantage of the opportunity to push the youth to his full potential. In the camp at night, he began to instruct Jeremiah on how to mix and bottle the potions and tonics he sold. Jeremiah seemed to enjoy the mixing and could easily recite the recipes when asked later.

Finimin was impressed with Jeremiah's energy and hunger to learn. He figured that Jeremiah would be a fine candidate to sell the various mixtures and planned to have the youth stand nearby with several bottles in hand, ready to exchange for cash, whenever he began his spiel to the crowd. With the two of them at the ready, each would be ready to coax a potential buyer into handing over his money. One day, after making some profitable sales, Finimin purposefully escorted Jeremiah to a mercantile and paid for a complete outfit of clothes for his new assistant, which was a cheap, off-the-shelf broadcloth suit, a cotton shirt, and a pair of low-heeled boots, along with a derby hat. 'A man in our profession needs to look the part,' Finimin explained.

When not selling or camping, Finimin would never pass up an out-of-the-way roadhouse or gambler's tent. George Finimin fancied himself as a gambler; a profession he preferred, but was not very good at. He had a propensity for drinking too much rotgut whiskey when he should have been giving his undivided attention to the game. George would get drunk then make wild bets and lose whatever money he had on the table or in his pockets. Becoming a seller of not-very-well-known, supposedly medicinal, potions happened because George, who shunned physical labor, needed to eat.

It did not take Jeremiah long to note that Finimin exaggerated the curative qualities of his products in order to make a sale, but Jeremiah had to eat too. Tagging along with the huckster seemed to be the thing to do. It was even kind of fun. The man had a practiced answer for anything asked and Jeremiah soon learned that the man tailored and fabricated his answers to leave anyone asking scratching his head. Finimin continually stretched the truth about most everything – his lineage, his age, the promised curatives of the potions he hawked, and his questionable past, which included claims to have studied medicine at the University of Providence, wherever that was. Jeremiah figured George would lie to his own grandmother to make a sale.

Finimin possessed an uncommon skill as an orator and was a convincing thespian. Whenever he located a gathering of people, he would stand on the seat of his carriage to summon attention to himself and the wares he offered. He would then begin an oratory about the curative qualities inside the little bottles he held aloft for all to see.

'Ladies and gentlemen, I am here only to help you out of your miseries. The price of the remedies I am offering, a mere pittance you will agree, is money spent wisely for your deserved relief,' he would say dramatically. When he had a group of wide eyed-listeners gawking at him, he would hold up a Bible. 'Sometimes I feel that I've been sent here by the Almighty to bring healing to you folks.'

That always did it, and eager hands would hold out dollar bills or coins. George Finimin could have been a preacher and would have made a good one, but he was too much of a sinner himself. After the final sale of the day, Finimin chose to spend the rest of the night gambling, whoring and drinking to excess – that is, when he had the money.

Jeremiah had learned well from George never to pass up an opportunity to extract money from the unsuspecting; dealing lowly, if the need called for it.

'You have to be quick on your feet. Strike while the iron is still hot!' George would announce. 'Don't worry about a few white lies spoken, we'll be gone tomorrow. Do what you have to do to get the money, while you can, before the opportunity is lost.'

It did not take long for Jeremiah, no stranger to hard times, to acquire the intuitiveness to feel and know when trouble was brewing. Finimin often created an atmosphere of distrust wherever they traveled. At times Jeremiah would attempt to persuade Finimin to go easy on spending his money, usually to no avail. Jeremiah had hauled George Finimin's whiskey-soaked carcass out of many a tent or low-class saloon, after George had gambled away what money he had in his pockets. At times, if one or more disgruntled locals began to complain about Finimin's claims of miracle cures then Jeremiah would make sure the mule was ready to make a hasty retreat. When things got hot, Jeremiah would whisk George out of town, when both of them were on the verge of receiving a coating of tar and feathers.

If anyone pressed George for credentials for services as a medical doctor, George would reply that he was merely presenting the finest of remedies, recommended by doctors. Said doctors were, apparently, a secret for he did not provide names.

'But you have a sign on your wagon that says you are a doctor,' an irritated man said.

Finimin replied, 'And that I am, a doctor of pharmaceutical mixtures recognized by leading physicians.' He would attempt to close the discussion by saying that he could not give medical advice. However, in out of the way places he did so anyway and often erroneously.

CHAPTER 3

At first Finimin paid for all of Jeremiah's needs, then one night in camp, six months after their joining, Jeremiah complained of not having a nickel to his name. At first Finimin thought the young man ungrateful, then, upon reflection of Jeremiah's worth to his business, he reconsidered and figured that Jeremiah had indeed become invaluable to him. Jeremiah did most of the camp labors and he was good at collecting the money held aloft for the bottles offered. Finimin himself would not like going around without at least some change in his pocket to buy, say, a cigar. He settled the issue by offering to cut Jeremiah in to ten percent of the profits of the business after showing Jeremiah the records of the cost of the products, theirs and Chelsea's needs and traveling expenses. The arrangement seemed to work out well. George paid Jeremiah at the end of each sales session and Jeremiah never questioned what he was paid or asked for a raise.

During their time together, Jeremiah had learned a great deal about George Finimin. In Jeremiah's mind, Finimin, though lazy, was not such a bad person. The man was predictable, a bit pompous and vain, trusting to no one, and had forged a way just short of stealing to make a living. He had no roots, never mentioning having any relatives or a home life, and preferred being mobile.

Strangers bought the various mixtures Finimin offered and sold as a last-ditch effort for theirs or a loved one's pain, fully hopeful that the claimed cure-all would alleviate a chronic condition. In some too far-gone cases, only a physician or an undertaker could be of service. For that reason, some folks would purposely avoid him while others would hail him from a distance.

Most of the potions that Finimin offered were mixtures of his own making, using his own recipes, and would, unbeknownst to the purchaser, do nothing for the recipient, other than to be a bitter experiment. He did carry and offered for sale some items commonly known and prescribed by those in the medical field such as Castor Oil, Paregoric and peppermint for mild cases of children's maladies. When he sold other stronger potions, like quinine, Croton oil or Laudanum for those that had a chronic condition or were terminally ill, he took the time to be very specific to the person buying the product, instructing them to take charge and oversee the patient's dosage.

Other items carried included bag balm for burns, small bottles of tincture of arnica used for sprains and bruises, or his own concoction of red pepper liniment, which he promised would give immediate relief. He also stocked a small supply of chewing tobacco, snuff and cheap cigars. He bought caseload quantities of various substances, in small bottles, housed in a wooden box, from a jobber's warehouse in St Louis, paying cash for the goods with no questions asked. He priced each bottle of the various mixtures so that he at least tripled his money from each sale.

The real money, though, was in the homemade nostrums that he mixed up. His liniment was a concoction of oil of wintergreen and camphor oil. Almost anyone could have mixed the concoction at home. Finimin, however, had a little twist to the recipe. At night in camp, he would bring the ingredients to a boil then throw in a couple dried Mexican red peppers for added warmth and a little alcohol for each eight-ounce bottle that he corked. His cost was 3 to 5 cents and he sold each small bottle for a dollar. Stomach powders were nothing more than repackaged baking soda at 25 cents a dose. For ladies' monthly miseries, there were small tins of dried tealeaves, labeled 'Ladies Tea', that were snatched up at 1000 percent profit.

His best-selling item was 'Dr Finimin's Golden Flixir' that was emblazoned on his carriage. George would not admit to anyone that the empty bottle cost more than the ingredients that went into it. In a night time camp, he would mix up enough ingredients to fill two dozen small bottles. In a large pot, he would begin by pouring in a quantity of grain alcohol then throw in a couple sticks of black rank tobacco for color, a small Mexican red pepper for a memorable taste and a peppermint stick for refreshment. When done boiling, he would pour the mixture through a strainer, and then add creek water for volume. The result was a golden-colored mixture that he bottled up and would offer for sale at a dollar a bottle.

George Finimin often made good sales but his night time wasteful habits ensured that, no matter how much he pocketed in cash, the accounting the next morning revealed barely enough to pay living expenses. He was on occasion mistakenly thought to be a medical doctor, and called on to administer relief by a distraught relative of the ailing. George Finimin would let the messenger know that he was merely a peddler, but would look at the stricken. He would see the person, usually bed ridden, and recommend some tonic or other, which he just happened to have in his carriage. Afterwards he would advise that the person continued to rest. There was no law against Finimin mixing and selling his concocted remedies. In fact, on rare occasions, some folks may have actually benefited from the concoctions. Nevertheless Finimin did his best to be gone after a sale, figuring that by the time he made another visit, perhaps folks' memory would have softened if not failed.

He was cautious whenever he approached a lonely farmhouse, mentally noting if the place was prosperous or run down. If things seemed orderly, then he would drive up to the front of the house, climb down, swing up a hinged side of the boxed carriage and prop it open with a broomstick. When he had the goods displayed to his liking, he would then go into a practised sales pitch, all the while passing out some boiled sweets to any children that usually came out first. The woman of the house usually followed. If of childbearing age, she would briefly ogle the goods then reach for a tin of 'Ladies Tea' or a bottle of liniment.

The older women usually reached for a bottle of 'Mrs. Douglas's Choice' – the label proclaiming it a laxative offering 'fast gentle relief', which was nothing more than croton oil placed into a small bottle with a colorful label. Small packages of stomach powders (baking soda), purposely displayed nearby offered relief of gas pains. Bottles of Paregoric and Castor oil were easy enough to sell, when Finimin prodded a little. Yellow-backed dime novels, some showing previous thumbing, sold well. He read them at night in his many isolated camps before selling as new, being careful to not bend the pages.

If, however, the home site looked neglected, Finimin would merely ask to water his mule or perhaps offer to tinker by sharpening some knives or do some kind of work in exchange for a meal.

Finimin never told others his next destination and did not hold to a specific route. Often he would turn the carriage south when he had been steadily heading east for a lengthy time. Whether he was merely capitalizing on his own intuition or putting distance behind them in fear of some sort of dissatisfaction with the products, he did not disclose.

CHAPTER 4

It was late, close to midnight in the darkened camp, before Jeremiah was able to sit up and take stock in the realization of what had transpired earlier that evening. He rolled over to his hands and knees then stood. He knew that George was dead, but he stepped to the man's side anyway, suppressing a gorge at the grizzly bloody sight of the ruined body in the moonlight. He breathed deeply then stooped to rake his hand over George's eyes to close them. The overturned carriage was likely ruined, but any salvage would have to wait until daylight. If he could get it back on its wheels, hopefully he would have a means to leave this miserable place. For now, the only thing he could do was to cover Finimin's remains with a blanket and throw some limbs on the almost dead fire. It would be daylight before he could dig a grave for George.

The shooting gave Jeremiah reason for contemplation. Old George had been Jeremiah's mentor, taking him in when others had shunned the youth. In the three years spent with the man, Jeremiah had never witnessed Finimin purposefully intending harm to anyone's person. The finagling the man did to get his hands on someone's money was not reason to kill him. The man had numerous faults, but did not deserve to die at the hands of strangers who had killed him as if he were a stray dog.

Jeremiah had never been prone to violence while living with his mother and father. Later on, he had gotten his first taste of rough treatment by his Uncle Charles's belt in his outrage over Jeremiah's supposed misconduct. He held no plans to get even with his uncle – hell, that was just part of growing up. In one respect, how his uncle had treated him had toughened the youth. After he left his uncle's farm, he found most folks, including George Finimin, acted kindly toward him and he had no reason to resort to violence himself.

The heartless murder of George Finimin, however, brought matured feelings to the young man. He had immediately hardened and for the first time in his life felt the urge to retaliate in kind. Right now, nothing seemed more important than avenging George's death. Jeremiah's mind was active as he began formulating a plan. He would take George's old shotgun from the carriage, if it was still there, and go after those cowardly bastards; he knew where the killer's farm was located. Though he had never caused physical harm to anyone, he felt that he could pull the trigger on the shooter without any compunction and he was mad enough to do it. To him it would be no more than shooting a rabid fox or skunk. The bastards deserved to die.

He reasoned that if he did hunt down and kill the shooter, the other man, who had saved him from a shotgun blast, would alert authorities but he did not care. The emblazoned carriage, if he could salvage it, would be a beacon for anyone to locate. He figured that if he did find and managed to shoot the killer, he would have to contend with the others, the younger ones as well, but that did not deter him from his plans. They had murdered George and disrupted the only life that Jeremiah knew.

They had exacted their form of retribution and he would not rest until he had retaliated in kind. 'An eye for an eye,' the one man had said.

Jeremiah lit a lantern, then rummaged through the overturned carriage until he found the twin-barreled shotgun and broke it open. It was loaded. He found a box of extra shells, slipping half a dozen shells into his jacket pockets.

Jeremiah began walking toward the farm, which lay to the east about two miles away.

Eventually, he came to a halt in a grove of gum trees some 200 yards from the farmhouse, which sat in a clearing. He was facing the building, which had two front windows, one on either side of door. The place was darkened, most likely everyone inside was asleep at this hour. A covered wagon stood off to the right next to a barn. Before it the remnants of a campfire had died down to a few glowing embers. He could see the bulky figures of three men lying under blankets near the fire. He figured Emil Croft the killer to be the one lying near to the side of the wagon and the two younger men who had beaten himself and George before firing their pistols into George's lifeless body to be the ones closer to the fire.

Jeremiah stared at the three lying on the ground, studying them. He wanted to take out the older man first but if the two younger ones got in the way, he would not hesitate to shoot them as well. They had proved they were as heartless as their father and in need of extermination. He pondered how to go about the killing. The shotgun held two shots but there were three of them. He could easily get two of them but was not sure he could reload in time to get the third one, if he had to and then there was the possibility of Harold Menning's intervention to consider. He leaned his back to an ash tree while he contemplated.

He breathed deeply; no time like the present, he figured, nothing to gain by waiting and he wanted to get this over with tonight. Jeremiah cocked both the shotgun's hammers then stepped toward the glow of the campfire where the men lay in their bedding. He extended the shotgun's muzzle to bear on the man lying closest to the wagon, the one he figured to be Emil Croft. He wanted to be sure of his intended target before he pulled the trigger. His conscience would not allow him to pull the trigger on an unidentified target.

Jeremiah thought perhaps one of them would awaken and sound the alarm but no one moved. He reached one hand down and grasped a piece of wood then tossed it onto the fire. A few sparks rose in the night like fireflies. The thump caused Clarence Croft, the older of the two brothers to sit up. It took Clarence a few moments before recognition came to him. He pointed a finger at Jeremiah. 'You!' he yelled, then made a move to his middle for a gun or a knife as he attempted to rise. Jeremiah tripped a trigger on the shotgun. The blast caught Clarence Croft in the middle of his chest, flinging him back with a spray of blood and pieces of tissue painting the side of the wagon. A knife from his hand was flung away in his death throes.

When the other younger man, stunned by the noise, sat up near the fire, Jeremiah rushed forward to slam the stock of the shotgun to his head, just as he tried to dodge the blow. It was a hard blow making a thump like hitting a melon. A six-gun lay near the man's blankets but he had made no move to grasp it. Either he was too stunned or too stupid to do so. The hit of the gunstock slamming on to the side of his head caused the now inert man to fall onto his back, his legs twitching.

Jeremiah, in the surrounding darkness, knew he had mistaken Clarence lying in his blankets to be his father

27

Emil. Too late now as he swung the muzzle to his right but Emil was too quick. At the sound of the shotgun blast, the man had awakened and rolled from his blankets then crabbed away on hands and knees into the darkness. The movement caught Jeremiah unable to react to the movement while dealing with the younger brother. Jeremiah swung the shotgun to where Emil had disappeared. He caught a glimpse of movement in the moonlit shadows and pulled the second trigger of the shotgun. He heard Emil yelp in pain as some of the pellet shot struck his upper legs and back. Jeremiah heard thrashing in the leaves and brush as the man ran away, and cursed that the distance had been too great for the shot to have full effect.

Jeremiah dropped to a knee, broke open the shotgun, ejecting the empties then reached into his jacket pocket for fresh shells. He hurriedly slid them into the tubes and snapped the breech closed.

He looked about cautiously, expectant of a gunshot from who-knows-where. He did not know if Emil was armed or not, but nothing happened. Just then yellow lamplight spilled through a rectangular window. Jeremiah tensed, shotgun at the ready, then began stepping cautiously toward the front door. A woman's voice called to him, pleading, 'Mister, please don't shoot anymore. We don't need this violence in what life the Lord has left for Harold and me to live out.'

'Show yourself!' Jeremiah commanded, 'I promise I will not shoot you.'

After a minute of silence, the front door cracked a few inches then pushed fully open to reveal a woman in nightclothes.

Jeremiah held the shotgun in both hands, both hammers eared back as he stared at the woman standing in the doorway, but did not point the weapon at her.

'Where is your man?' Jeremiah asked, 'I mean you and him no harm.'

'He's right here,' the woman stammered. 'I won't let him come out. He told me what happened to you and the older man. Harold said that he had no part of it, tried to talk Emil out of it before they even got there. I recognize you as one of the ones came to see Maggie and we are not faulting you for what you just did to them after what they did out there in your camp.'

'They came to our camp, beat me unconscious and murdered my friend, a good man,' Jeremiah informed her. 'I came here to exact some retribution just like they claimed to be doing earlier.'

The woman nodded her head, 'Harold told me all about it. I am surprised that they did not kill you too, but you have to understand that Harold would not hurt anyone. He didn't even want to go along but felt he should.'

Jeremiah nodded, 'The reason I am not after Harold is because he stopped those others from killing me too.' He paused a moment, 'The one I wanted to shoot was Emil. I put some pellets in him but I heard him running away. Is he your relative, ma'am?'

The woman shook her head, 'He was married to my sister for a time when they were both very young, but then he turned out so mean that she left him after six months. The two boys are his by a second marriage. The three of them are thieves and murderers, no goods. Harold said that they had a homestead up in north-western Kansas, but left it and are now on the run from some horrible deeds they did in that area. They have no place to call their own so they came here, hiding out, I suppose. They have been here ten days; brought Emil's current wife, the third one, poor Maggie, here to die. We put her to rest this morning.

29

I was in hopes they all would leave, but Harold did not know how to ask them to move on without causing ill-will. Harold and I both thought it was just terrible what they did and I prayed for you and the man they killed.'

'I shot one of them dead,' Jeremiah admitted. 'Then I clubbed the other one; might have killed him too. Emil, the killer, got away into the night but I intend to catch up to him.'

The woman nodded, 'If it's Judson the younger one you clubbed, don't trouble yourself over him. He only did what his father and older brother told him to do. He's a little slow in the head.'

Jeremiah nodded, 'I'll take your word for that, ma'am, but he's not the one that I am after. It's Emil Croft that I want and when I see him again, I will kill him.'

The woman stared with eyes wide. 'Oh my,' she said, 'If I know Emil for what he has shown himself to be, in what time that he has been here, he cares for no one but himself. If he took off running then he most likely will not come back, even at the cost of his two no-account sons' lives. I heard him telling Harold that his sons had become a hindrance to the way he wanted to live. He was looking for a way to run them off so that he would not have to fend for them any longer. As soon as he could, he intended to get back to where they had come from and start a new life, which we both figured was a life of crime. The wagon and mules he left aren't worth his coming back to claim.'

Jeremiah felt bad for causing this seemingly good woman trouble, but her voice was strong, and protecting her man the way she did gave Jeremiah cause for respect. She dismissed him by saying, 'Harold and I will see to Clarence and Judson and take care of the burying. I'm sure you would like to put some distance from here.'

Jeremiah nodded, 'Understood, ma'am, I'll be on my

way but I intend to make Emil Croft pay for killing my friend.'

Exhausted as he felt, Jeremiah walked into the darkness in the direction that Emil Croft had run. His hope was to find the man and finish him. However, it was not to be. The darkness made it impossible to track the man so, after a short time of straining to see, he headed back to his own camp. He kept the shotgun ready, wary that Emil Croft might come busting out of a shadow and bushwhack him.

CHAPTER 5

Once back in camp, without incident, Jeremiah kindled a campfire then put coffee on to boil while he searched and found a shovel in the carriage wreckage. He then sat by the fire with the shotgun nearby, patting his face with a cloth soaked in canteen water. At the first hint of light in the east, he began digging a grave in a peaceful looking spot under a large hickory tree.

When finished burying George, he stood silently, with shovel in hand, staring at the mound for a few moments. Jeremiah, still in a distressed state, could not think of anything to say over the man's final resting place other than to mutter, 'Rest in peace, George.' He then turned his attention to the carriage and studied how to get it upright. He fashioned some rigging, using ropes, with one end secured to a gum tree, then coaxed Chelsea to pull the carriage upright. When the carriage was back on its four wheels, it looked as if things were not as bad as he had first thought. The carriage appeared to be in decent enough condition to roll again. Though the left rear wheel wobbled some, it did not rub. On inspection of the carriage contents, he found that much of the bottled goods were still intact. He busied himself throwing out the broken ones, then salvaged everything worthwhile. As he worked on the goods, he had thoughts of Harold Menning possibly alerting the authorities. Under the circumstances, he did not think the man would but if he did, then so be it.

Jeremiah felt no remorse for his taking action against the Crofts. He was not particularly worried, but still he kept the shotgun nearby as he finished the chores. Now that it was light, he fought off the impulse to go on a search until he found Emil Croft and finish him off. In reality, he figured that Croft had retreated to a distance to lick his wounds. Locating the man would be a feat of luck. He resigned himself to the fact that maybe it would be best to put the vengeance of George's death temporarily behind him and just leave. Someday his and Croft's paths were destined to cross again. Croft could change his name and run but that did not stop the fact that Jeremiah would remember the man's face forever. He would be on the lookout and not hesitate to kill the man in that eventuality.

It was mid-afternoon by the time Jeremiah finished cleaning and loading the usable remnants of the camp. After hitching Chelsea to the carriage, he then stepped onto the rig, seated himself, then snapped the reins to get Chelsea moving. After a short distance, Jeremiah pulled Chelsea to a stop. He was exhausted from all the happenings of the past twenty-four hours and knew that he was not thinking straight. Being this close, he was not about to leave the area until he had given a daylight search for Emil Croft; maybe the wounded man had left a blood trail that could be followed.

He moved about a mile away to set up a different camp. He quickly unhitched Chelsea then gave her a generous portion of oats. He rubbed her down with a gunnysack while she munched.

33

Knowing she would not wander far, he left her without tether to drink or forage as she saw fit. He was too tired to kindle a fire so he rolled up in a blanket under the carriage and immediately fell asleep.

Jeremiah woke up as the first light of the next morning began to illuminate his camp. He was refreshed, but still groggy. He lay for a few minutes reflecting on what had transpired the day before. He then rolled from under the carriage and stood up. In a short time he had a fire going and put the coffee pot on then turned his attention to Chelsea. She eagerly began feeding on the grain he had put in a nosebag. He then fried bacon and a pancake for his own breakfast. Afterwards, he sat supping coffee and contemplated the fact that Emil Croft might still be around so he would look to make sure. He hobbled Chelsea so that she would not wander after him, then picked up the shotgun and some extra shells and headed toward the Menning farm.

Jeremiah took the time to look around, studying the area so that he could find his way back. He took the shotgun and some extra shells then set off on foot back toward the Mennings' farm. He did not want nor need to talk to anyone so he skirted the buildings. He did come close enough to see two fresh graves mounded in the red clay of an open field, confirming the hit he had given to Judson's head was fatal. Obviously, the Mennings had seen to things just as the woman had said.

Jeremiah worked his way around until he got as close as he dared to where the wagon was parked. He found a small amount of blood spotting some leaves on the ground where Emil had fled, but the blood trail lasted only a few feet then there was none. He searched the area for tracks or blood splotches for an hour but found nothing. With no sign of Croft, it was evident that the man was not too badly wounded and could be miles away by now. He pondered whether to go to the Mennings to see if Emil came back, but figured that since Mrs Menning had said he most likely would not, he decided against it.

It was past noon by the time he got back to his camp. He made a sandwich of bacon and bread, washing it down with canteen water. His mind wandered as he ate. He had killed the two brothers, who were partially responsible for George's death. He felt no remorse for his actions and was unconcerned that Harold Menning might go to the authorities. The woman would most likely change her husband's mind to keep quiet, but if not, then so be it; he would deal with whatever transpired. He also doubted that Emil Croft would turn to the law regarding his sons' deaths; after all, Emil had murdered George and would not be able to justify his actions if asked. Mrs Menning had said Emil was both a thief and a murderer and wanted for some past crimes, but most likely would head back to where he had come from. Jeremiah sighed in disgust when he realized that he had not asked where that was. Mrs Menning had said Emil's homestead was in north-western Kansas, but had not said specifically where. Jeremiah had never been to Kansas but figured it covered a large area. Eventually he would have to go there to find out.

He had no idea how he would go about hunting the man down but no matter what, he would not rest until he found and dealt with Emil Croft. For now, the thing to do was to make tracks. He brushed breadcrumbs off his front then hitched Chelsea to the carriage and headed out.

As he drove along, he thought about the future. For the immediate, other than putting some miles behind him, he had no choice but to keep on doing what he and George had done, which was to scratch out a living by selling potions. It would be a while before he would attempt to

35

find a likely customer and exhibit the wares as usual. He had no plan to hold public orations, hawking the products like George had done; he would just make the carriage and himself visible and let the goods sell themselves. He would simply arrive at a homestead or likely small-town street corner and let the advertising on the wagon draw interest. If anyone were to start asking medical advice, let them, he could not give what he did not know; he was just a traveling peddler. If a potential customer asked what the potion was supposed to do for them, of course he would go into one of Finimin's practised recitals but guarantee nothing.

As slipshod as the business was, Jeremiah considered that he had merely stepped in to run the business when George Finimin had departed, however untimely. Perhaps under Jeremiah's management, with subtle changes to the way the goods were presented for sale, he might just turn a profit better than George had ever done.

CHAPTER 6

It was November and fall was evident with brown leaves littering the ground. Finimin had driven south to escape the colder temperatures in the north. Nights were cold and the ground was frosty in the mornings. For some days, the only sale he had made was a tinned container of powdered snuff to a farmer who said he was glad Jeremiah came by because he had a lingering tobacco hunger and his supply had run out.

It was now years after the war, but it appeared that those poor folks he visited had not recovered from the effects of the plunder done to the land. He did not feel at ease in the land of his birth and recognized that nothing much had changed since he had left his uncle's farm some four years previous, and he was not about to pay his uncle a visit.

In his travels, he found that everyone was waiting for their crops to come in before they could spare a dime. There were, however, plenty of beans, corn bread and turnip greens happily served to the wandering peddler. With so little cash money available, he had no choice but to keep on traveling north, back to the familiar areas that he and Finimin had worked before. It took him an entire week to travel through his home state of Arkansas and he was not sorry to leave. When he had left the first time, it was in hopes to find a new life. He had done that thanks to George Finimin, but this second visit had ended in disaster. Jeremiah stayed very mobile in his travel and avoided farms along the way. He really did not feel like talking to strangers right now. He just wanted to leave this part of the country and start out fresh at some other location.

His northern route had taken him some forty miles south-west of Springfield, Missouri, when that wobbly left rear wheel began to rub the side of the carriage body. Chelsea stopped her progress by the drag of the wheel and turned her head to look at her master. Jeremiah got down then jacked the rear end of the carriage up and rotated the wheel, which wobbled badly. He did not have the tools or the know-how to make repairs. It was obvious that he needed the expertise of a blacksmith. A half hour ago, he had passed by a forlorn looking dilapidated farmhouse. He had not stopped by because at a distance the place looked so bad he did not feel the residents would even be able to provide a meal. Now he had no choice but to see if perhaps somehow, whoever lived there might be willing to offer assistance or advice about the wheel.

Jeremiah coaxed Chelsea into turning around and they headed back to the farmhouse. The wheel still rolled but rubbed, seeming worse than before.

The house, barn and other outbuildings were situated on a pleasant flat surrounded by cottonwood trees, and looked to be more than a few years old. The site, however, did little to disguise the rundown appearance of the buildings. The house, weathered to gray, looked sturdy enough but a few loosened shingles on the roof spoke of neglect. The barn off to the left had a saggy roof. A lean-to next to the barn had a badly leaning outside post and looked as if it were near to falling over. The corral surrounding the lean-to had two top poles where one end had fallen to the ground. A milk cow and a mule occupied a small pasture behind the barn. In the yard fronting the house, a dozen speckled chickens were busy pecking the ground.

A large tan colored mutt came off the elevated front porch of the house then stood in the yard barking at the intrusion. Jeremiah brought Chelsea to a halt at about twenty yards from the front of the house. The mutt did not appear aggressive, but Jeremiah sat his seat until the front door opened and a slight, balding older-looking man wearing bib overalls stepped out with a walking cane in hand. A thin woman stood in the doorway behind the man. 'That's enough, Duke,' the man yelled at the dog, which quieted immediately.

Jeremiah figured it was safe to step down. 'I don't mean to bother you, sir, but a wheel on my carriage is out of round and rubbing the carriage. I am in need of repairs, but I have no tools. I am able to pay for any assistance you are able to spare.'

The man turned to the woman and they spoke in hushed tones. He then turned back to face Jeremiah, 'We will be happy to oblige you with what we can, mister. No need to speak of payment.'

Jeremiah nodded then stepped forward and extended a hand to the man. 'The name is Jeremiah Hackett. I am traveling up to Independence.'

The man, perhaps sixty years or older, grasped Jeremiah's hand, 'Clovis Blanchard,' he thumbed a hand over his shoulder, 'my wife Millie.' The woman, perhaps twenty years younger had a pleasant face accentuated by a smile. Her hair pulled tight in a bun was almost brown, but streaked with gray. She nodded, 'Pleased to meet you, Jeremiah.'

Clovis flared a hand, 'We were about to have a noon meal. We do not get many visitors and you are welcome to join us. Millie said to invite you. She said she has cooked up enough to feed all of us.'

Jeremiah nodded and smiled, 'I am plenty hungry and tired of my own cooking. I'd surely like to see to my little mule first, if you don't mind.'

Clovis nodded, 'I like a man who is considerate of his animals. You can go ahead and unhitch the critter, if you want. There is a trough over by that lean-to barn. Hay and water, you're welcome to come on in the house when you are ready.'

The inside of the house was neat and clean, a far cry from the neglected conditions outside.

Clovis had seated himself at a table surrounded by four chairs. A red and white checkered oilcloth covered the tabletop.

'Have a seat Jeremiah. Everything is ready,' Millie said as she set a cake of cornbread on the table. Jeremiah hung his hat on a straight back chair then took a seat.

The meal was simple, beans, boiled potatoes, turnip greens and cornbread and sweet pickles. Clovis picked up a porcelain pitcher and offered it to Jeremiah, 'Buttermilk?' The three-people quieted while they filled their plates then began eating.

'Guess you seen that things are a little neglected outside, Jeremiah,' Millie stated.

'Takes a fair amount of work to keep things in order at every home,' Jeremiah offered.

Millie pointed a fork at her husband, 'Clovis has always taken really good care of things but after he broke his leg, it's pretty rough on him to do heavy work.'

The three chatted for half an hour after the meal. Jeremiah told of his potion business and need to fix the carriage wheel.

Clovis nodded, 'John Hughes, our closest neighbor has a forge, and has fixed a few things for us in the past. I know he will fix it for you and will not charge you an arm and a leg. I'll go with you if you want.' He pointed to his left, 'About two miles down that path. You can hitch up our mule and wagon; take your wheel to him. Millie will look out for your stuff. No one will bother things here.'

Jeremiah spent an hour taking the wheel off the carriage then loaded it onto Clovis' wagon. Then he and Clovis took the wheel to Hughes's farm. After Clovis and Hughes gave each other a greeting, Clovis introduced Jeremiah then explained about the wheel.

Hughes, a barrel-shaped friendly man gripped Jeremiah's hand firmly.

He inspected the wheel, took one hand and lifted a floppy-brimmed hat and scratched his head then let the hat fall back on his head. 'I expect I can fix it. Have to take the spokes off then heat up the rim and pound it back into shape. It might be a day or so before I can work on it. I've got some other blacksmithing work to do ahead of yours.' He turned to Jeremiah, 'You staying over at Clovis' place?'

Clovis answered for him, 'Yes he is, John. We'll check in with you in a few days.'

It was near dark by the time they got back to the Blanchards' place. Jeremiah stopped the wagon in front of the house, then helped Clovis down to the ground. 'I'll take care of the wagon and the mule,' Jeremiah said.

'Come to the house when you're done,' Clovis said, 'Millie most likely has supper waiting.'

During the meal, Jeremiah reiterated his thanks for the help. 'I'll take care of some of those outside chores in the morning,' he offered.

Millie nodded, 'You are welcome, young man. Do not

worry any about being a burden to us. We could surely use some outside help, but you need not feel obligated. We'll get by.'

Jeremiah nodded, 'Would it be alright if I sleep in the barn?'

Millie shook her head side to side, 'It's too cold out there. We have an extra room. It was our son Eddie's room. You can sleep there. Eddie hasn't been here to use it for near on two years now.'

Jeremiah spent the next three days doing badly needed repair work, which included replacing some shingles on the roof of the house and fixing the roof of the lean-to so that it was straight again, then he went to work on the corral fencing. He would begin each day before breakfast by seeing that Chelsea, the milk cow and the Blanchards' mule had food and water. He then milked the cow and fed the chickens. After breakfast, he would set to work on the repairs.

At near dark of the third night, Clovis called from the front door, 'Supper is ready, Jeremiah.'

Jeremiah washed up then went inside. Clovis sat at the table, 'We'll go check on your wheel tomorrow, Jeremiah.'

The next morning Jeremiah hitched the mule to the wagon then drove over to the house to get Clovis. John Hughes had seen them coming in the distance and rolled the now repaired carriage wheel out through the open bay doors of the barn as they drove up. He stood holding the wheel up while grinning. 'I finished it yesterday. I was going to bring it out to you today, but you saved me having to hitch my wagon up.'

After loading the wheel into Clovis' wagon, Jeremiah stated his appreciation for fixing the wheel and happily handed Hughes two dollars; the man's stated fee for the job.

Back at Blanchard's place, Clovis stood to watch as Jeremiah put the wheel on the freshly greased hub, then spun it to watch it rotate around in perfect alignment.

Jeremiah spent the rest of the day working around the place. He figured to do all the work he could today and be on his way early tomorrow. At supper, Jeremiah told the man and woman of his intent to leave in the morning.

Millie stared at him for a moment then said, 'I, uh, we wish that you wouldn't do that, Jeremiah. We know that you have things to see to, but it is too cold out for you to be traipsing off trying to sell your stuff. Most folks are sitting tight and just trying to keep warm. Clovis and I had a talk about it and we would like you to stay here with us at least through the winter. We can't pay you a wage, but as you know there's plenty of food and a warm place to sleep.'

Jeremiah was happily surprised. What Millie was offering made sense. He had no problem avoiding night-time cold camps. On top of that, he was not apt to be able to make any volume of potion sales until he reached Independence, and even doing that depended on the weather. There would not be many travelers to sell to until spring.

Jeremiah spent the next four months with Clovis and Millie. During that time, Millie told him about how they were heartbroken when their son left to find his fortune. Eddie fell into bad company and ran afoul with the law. He was currently serving a five-year term in prison for a hold-up that went sour. She had hoped that when his sentence was up he would return home, but she no longer believed that he would. 'Once an apple goes bad, there's no way to make it fresh again,' she said with disdain.

Since Millie had laid bare her and Clovis' life, Jeremiah

in turn told of how he got into potion selling. He told of how George Finimin was murdered and how he in turn had retaliated and killed the two younger Croft boys. He told how it was his intent to find Emil Croft and kill him.

Millie listened intently then said, 'I'm mighty sorry to hear of your troubles, Jeremiah, but I understand completely. You have to do what you feel is right however long it takes. As long as you keep that in mind, I believe that things will work out.'

It was a bright spring morning in April when Jeremiah left the Blanchard farm. He was satisfied that the place was in better shape than when he arrived.

Business in Missouri began slowly, then greatly improved when he ventured into the frontier city of Independence some two weeks after leaving the Blanchard farm. Independence was a 'go to and come from' place; it seemed that everyone in town was heading to or coming from places out west. He did quite well offering his wares to crowds of pioneers, buffalo hunters, army personnel, railroad people and traveling pilgrims of all sorts.

CHAPTER 7

It was early October 1879, almost a year after George Finimin's death. At first, after leaving the Blanchards, Jeremiah's intent was to head into Kansas and hunt down Emil Croft. However, with the need to bring enough money in to sustain him and Chelsea, he had no choice but to put vengeance aside. He busied himself in preparation to do some potion sales business. Jeremiah, now twenty-two years old, had not forgotten George's death; fact is it came to mind every time he arrived at a new town. He would take the time to stop in at the local marshal or sheriff's office and inquire if they had any knowledge of Emil Croft. So far, he had learned nothing, but that did not deter him. He would keep asking, knowing that eventually he would get a lead on the man.

After leaving St Joseph, he headed east back toward St Louis. He liked St Louis. He figured to do the usual at this time of year, which was to stay at the Grand Hotel for a week or so and take a break from his life on the road. Afterwards, he would restock his inventory then head out again perhaps to Kansas. He had made good money in Independence and St Joseph, and was looking forward to a stay at the Grand. It was George, of course, who had first introduced him to the first-class place, which was clean

45

and quiet and served fine food; a welcome respite from trail camps. The hotel had its own stable to care for guests' animals. It took money to stay there but he had budgeted his finances well and figured he deserved the stay as it had been over a year since his last visit. He would love to spend the entire winter there, but money-wise that was out of the question. He looked forward to a nice weeklong stay before heading back out on the trail.

At the end of the day's travel eastward, he stopped in a little grove of cottonwoods to make a camp near a two-yard wide creek. Jeremiah cared for George's, now his, little hinny mare Chelsea. He rubbed her down with a gunny-sack and gave her a nosebag of corn. He had just finished his evening meal of boiled beans, cornbread and some strong coffee then sat smoking a stogie while he stared into the flames of his campfire as darkness was approaching.

Chelsea heard the noise before Jeremiah did, as she gave a little whinny out and stamped a foot in protest. Jeremiah looked over to her and noticed her ears were erect. That was when he started looking around and walked over to the carriage to be near the old double-barreled shotgun that rested below the seat. Right after George's death, he had kept the shotgun close by his person, wielding it in hand at the slightest noise. But now, after so long a time had passed and the fact that he had not suffered an occasion to make a show of the old shotgun, he had grown lax – perhaps too much so.

He did not take the shotgun in hand, but was comforted enough that it was within arms-reach.

Soon he could hear the hoof beats before he could make out the riders in the coming darkness. He was not worried that a disgruntled customer was coming to complain; he had not sold anything for four days and no strong mixtures at that.

The normal courtesy of a stranger coming to a stranger's camp was to call out a greeting from a short distance away. The two riders that approached said nothing as they rode up to face Jeremiah.

Jeremiah overlooked the intrusion and said, 'Evening.'

'Evening,' one of the men said, 'That coffee smells good.'

'Step down and help yourself to some,' Jeremiah offered while flaring a hand toward the pot near the campfire. The two riders looked to be wandering cowboys, their clothes dusty and wrinkled, both needful of a long overdue bath and a change of clothes. It seemed safe enough so Jeremiah relaxed, figuring the two were perhaps on their way home.

Both men dismounted and dropped their reins to the ground then walked to the campfire.

Jeremiah opened the back of the wagon and got two tin cups and plates out then stepped to hand them to the men. 'There's beans and cornbread there. I cooked enough for breakfast tomorrow but I can cook some more,' he offered. Both men nodded thanks and began to help themselves.

One man was tall and lean, his face appearing hawk-like. The other was a short, husky, fat-faced dirty-looking man with pig-like eyes. The tall one asked in between hurried bites. 'Where'd you come from, mister?'

'I come from St Jo and I'm headed over to St Louis on some business,' Jeremiah offered.

'When was that?' the tall one asked.

'You mean when did I leave St Jo? Well, that was two days hence.'

'Have you seen anybody on the trail since then?'

'Fact is, you men are the first I've seen since I left. Are

you looking for someone in particular?' Jeremiah asked.

'No, no, nothing like that, I was just curious, that's all. My name is Bill Ryan and this is Tucker Basham.' The short man bobbed his head, in agreement while continuing to eat. 'We're just on our way back to Jefferson City. We've been down to Sedalia for a spell.'

'I figured you were cowmen,' Jeremiah said.

'We got the look, eh?' the short one, Tucker Basham, said in a kind of sneering fashion.

'I didn't mean any offence by saying that you look like cowmen. There are a lot of men doing that kind of work in Missouri and other places from Mexico to Canada,' Jeremiah said.

'No offence taken,' Bill Ryan said. 'We're thankful for the grub. If you don't mind, we would be obliged if we could spend the night, seeing how you got a campfire and all. We'll be pushing on come first light.'

'Sure,' Jeremiah said, 'Spread your bedrolls up close to the fire, if you want. I generally sleep under the carriage, in case of sprinkles.'

Tucker Basham set his tin plate aside and refilled his coffee cup. He walked over and stood beside the carriage staring at the lettering. 'Are you this Doctor Finimin?'

'No, I am not. My name is Jeremiah Hackett and I just sell the doctor's products.'

'You're a peddler then!' Tucker Basham said gruffly and pointed his coffee cup at the lettering. 'Elixirs, potions and tonics, it says.' Jeremiah was surprised that the rough-looking man could read. 'You got any drinking tonics hidden in the carriage, peddler? I mean like whiskey?' he asked in a wishful way.

'I keep a bottle in the carriage for an occasional evening drink. I'd be happy to pour each of us a nightcap.' Jeremiah said then went to the side of the carriage and lifted a side. He reached inside and brought out a near-full bottle. He poured a generous amount in each of the men's cups and half as much in his own, then corked the bottle and set it in the open side of the carriage. He hoisted his cup, 'Here's to good days ahead.'

Bill Ryan acknowledged by raising his cup a little.

Tucker Basham made a sound that came out like, 'Harrumph,' as he stared into his cup. 'This here is fair rye whiskey,' he said, then downed the contents of his cup. He stepped over to the carriage then took up the bottle from within and poured his cup full. 'This bottle ain't gonna last long with three of us pulling on it. You got more in the box?' he asked.

'No, I don't,' Jeremiah said with a bit of apprehension. 'I generally carry only the one bottle.'

Bill Ryan stepped forward and filled his cup as well. In a short time, perhaps feeling the effects of the quickly-drank whiskey, Tucker Basham chuckled and said to Ryan, 'Did you hear that messenger squealing when I hit him?'

Ryan grinned broadly, 'I was too busy filling up my sack in the coaches. A young blonde woman in that second car started crying when I took her brooch; she was a sweet-looking pretty thing. I gave it back to her.'

'You did what!' Tucker exclaimed. 'If Jesse found out that you gave part of the loot back, he might deduct its worth from your share.'

'I saw him do the same thing, once before!' Ryan flared back.

The two standing drinkers seemed oblivious to Jeremiah being there at all. Jeremiah had seated himself to lean against a front wheel of the carriage. It sounded like they had robbed a train somewhere and he knew the more they drank, the more he would be in danger. He silently cursed himself for allowing the two strangers into camp unchallenged. He wondered if this would end in disaster as in the case of George Finimin's death. He was sure that he could rise unnoticed and retrieve the out of sight shotgun, but then what? There were two of them and he knew not their capabilities; some men were very accurate shooters, drunk or sober. Jeremiah figured it would be best to stay quiet for now.

Tucker Basham ended the seclusion, 'Hey peddler!' he laughed. 'This bottle's empty! You got alcohol and such in that box of yours. Why don't you mix us up a batch of something to drink!'

Bill Ryan turned toward Jeremiah, 'That's a great idea! I'll give you a hand.'

'I got some grain alcohol that isn't good for much but making liniment,' Jeremiah said and remained seated.

Tucker Basham drew his six-gun and pointed it at Jeremiah. 'We'll take it!' Tucker leered. When Jeremiah did not move, Basham cocked the six-gun. 'Go on, before I shoot you in the gizzard!'

'Put it away, Tuck!' Bill Ryan instructed. 'Someone might hear the shot.'

Jeremiah stood and held his hand palm down, in a calming effort, 'Hold on there, I'll get you something!' He went to the back of the carriage and opened a compartment under the watchful eye of Bill Ryan. Jeremiah pulled out a five-gallon keg and wrestled it to the tailgate.

'I've had grain alcohol before, it's mean stuff. What have you got to dilute it so's a man can drink it?' Ryan asked as he eyed the inside of the carriage.

'Water, coffee, maybe a little molasses,' said Jeremiah.

'We want something with a little kick,' Tucker giggled drunkenly.

Bill Ryan pointed to a bottle, 'What's that stuff?'

'Elixir,' Jeremiah said. 'Perhaps you might like the taste

of Doctor Finimin's Golden Elixir.' He held a bottle up for Ryan to see.

'Let's have a taste,' Ryan said. He took the bottle from Jeremiah and uncorked it, sniffed it then took a swallow, smacked his lips then said, 'Not bad, doc.'

He poured the rest of Finimin's Golden Elixir into his cup then had Jeremiah fill the cup up with half alcohol and half water. Ryan took a gulp, grimaced at the burn of the liquid going down his throat then hollered out, 'Whoa boy!'

Tucker, enlightened by Ryan's reaction to the mixture, rushed over with cup in hand, 'Hey, gimme some of that stuff!'

Jeremiah took a bottle of Golden Elixir and poured it into Tucker's cup, then filled the cup full with alcohol and water. Tucker took the cup. He gasped when he took a swallow, seemed to strangle, then went into a coughing fit. When he could talk again, he handed the empty whiskey bottle to Jeremiah. 'Mix us up a bottle full of that stuff.'

Both drinkers walked back to stand near the fire. Bill Ryan blurted out, 'Go ahead, peddler, fix us a good bottle. We may be a couple of train robbers, but we won't do you any harm, just as long as you keep the bar open!'

Jeremiah busied himself with the bottle, the alcohol, the Golden Elixir and some other ingredients that would remain a secret to the drinkers. When done, he presented the bottle to Tucker, and then took his seat against the carriage wheel again in a watchful position as the two giggled and drank.

'I'd say the rewards offered on us went up a tad bit the day after that robbery,' Tucker Basham laughed. 'You best watch it that I don't turn you in for the money, Bill.'

Bill Ryan frowned, 'That's a hell of a thing to say to your partner.'

Basham grinned, 'Just joking, buddy.'

After a long moment of silence, Basham began bragging a great deal more about their exploit. Neither of the men seemed to pay any attention to Jeremiah as they talked on as if he were not there. Before long, Jeremiah had gained the knowledge of which train they had robbed and where they were to meet up with the gang again. His interest was piqued by Basham's story about there being rewards offered.

CHAPTER 8

The next day it was near dark when Jeremiah stopped his carriage in front of the jail in Columbia. He got down and went inside. A few minutes later, a sheriff's deputy came outside with him. Behind Jeremiah's carriage were two saddle horses tied to the back of the carriage. Each horse pulled a travois drag made of blankets folded over sturdy cottonwood limbs. One travois carried Bill Ryan and the other carried Tucker Basham. Both men lay with their eyes closed. They appeared deathly-ill with a gray pallor to their faces. Jeremiah finished telling the story of their visit to his camp last night, but the deputy did not take much notice until he repeated the men's words bragging about the train robbery. The deputy got some help to haul the two men into cells on suspicion of being members of the James gang. Three nights ago, the gang had robbed a Chicago and Alton train at Glendale station, a number of miles away. Identifiable jewelry and some cash were found in both Ryan's and Basham's saddle-bags.

'I'm surprised that you got them,' the deputy said. 'A posse had been out searching the whole countryside since the night of the robbery. I don't know how those two managed to slip through. You'd think they would have high-tailed it out of the country before now. There will be a nice reward coming to you.'

Jeremiah, somewhat excited by the declaration asked, 'How much are they worth?'

'The last I heard, it was five hundred for each of the gang members,' the deputy replied.

After Dr Jonas Craig attended to the stricken men, he came into the jail's office and addressed Jeremiah. 'They said that you poisoned them. What did you give them?' he asked.

'Oh, it was just a little something to help clean their systems of the mixtures that they took from me and drank freely.'

'And what would that be?' Dr. Craig asked.

'Some of my finest mixtures including some Calomel with a large dose of Croton oil added!' Jeremiah smiled.

Dr Craig raised an eyebrow when he looked at Jeremiah, 'Good Lord, man! Croton oil is a powerful purgative used in small doses to induce vomiting and it is a hell of laxative to boot. One spoon of Calomel diluted in a glass of water will have the patient going at both ends inside of an hour.'

'I know, so I mixed two spoons into a quart bottle to make sure! Actually, it took a lot less than an hour for both of them to hit the bushes and then they spent the rest of the night running!'

'I'm surprised they didn't shoot you,' Dr Craig said. 'No one should be administering those drugs unless they are professionals. What you are doing is pure quackery.'

Jeremiah did not appear fazed by the implied insult, 'Both of them dropped their gun belts to the ground when they took off to relieve themselves. Once I had the guns, they were meek as lambs. Ryan asked if I could help him and Basham begged me to make it quit! I said I'd do what I could,' Jeremiah replied, 'So I brought them in.'

*

In a few days, Jeremiah collected a one-thousand-dollar reward from the railroad, five hundred for each of the bandits. Excited by the windfall, Jeremiah immediately went shopping, figuring it time to outfit himself in a more presentable fashion of his choice for the first time in his life. Starting from the ground up, he bought new calf-high boots, two pairs of gray pin-striped pants, a thigh-length black coat, a white shirt and a string tie, topped off with a low-crowned flat-brimmed black hat. He was glad to get rid of that awful derby that George had bought for him.

In his new attire, Jeremiah proceeded to the Grand Hotel in St Louis. He was comfortable with the hotel's livery seeing to Chelsea's care. The first few days he did little other than relax and take stock of his new wealth, which was the most money he had ever possessed, or seen for that matter, in his entire life. How he had acquired such a large amount of money so easily caused his mind to wonder. He had been getting by all this time on doing what he had learned from George Finimin, which was to sell potions. There was no prospect of making any significant gains. It was just a way to squeeze out a living. Now that he had made this large windfall by bringing those criminals in, he began to see things in a different light, which forever ended his get-by attitude to living. There were undoubtedly other wanted men with a price on their head roaming about, and he intended to look into seeing if he could manipulate himself into a position to pocket some of that reward money. He did not expect others to be as gullible as Bill Ryan and Tucker Basham, but then no-one ever made any headway without taking that first step.

That evening Jeremiah sipped on a glass of whiskey in

the Grand Hotel's bar while in deep thought. He now had enough of a stake to allow him to go on a sincere hunt for Emil Croft; maybe the rat had a bounty on his head. The very idea of bringing other wanted men in for bounty intrigued him as well. At times in his camp, those two robbers had given him cause for concern, but in the long run he had outwitted them, and then brought them in for the reward. Jeremiah's mind was active; he realised that as an amateur he would be prone to making mistakes, but why couldn't he, why shouldn't he find a way to bring others in? He was not bashful about bringing a wanted man in nor was he afraid of the prospect of facing one. The rewards he had received on Ryan and Basham sure beat squeaking out a living by selling potions. He felt compelled to give it a try, and perhaps get lucky and capture another wanted man. Satisfied that he had settled that issue, he reasoned that if he were to capitalize on this new way of making a lot of money, he would need to visit the local law constabulary. He would introduce himself and become familiar with what wanted posters they had on public display. He planned to do that first thing in the morning.

For tonight though, he figured to enjoy the fruits of his labor and try his hand at gambling. George had taught him how to play various poker hands in their nightly camps by betting dried beans or pebbles as the booty. It did not take Jeremiah long to figure out how to beat George at his own game and come out the winner. On top of that, he knew what not to do. When accompanying George to various saloons, he watched the man do OK until he had too many strong drinks under his belt; that was when he would make foolish bets that would leave him broke.

Jeremiah did not figure on following in George's exact

footsteps. He made up his mind that he would restrict any drinking other than having an occasional beer before gaming and coffee only while gambling. He cautiously entered a small stakes game to get a feel for the game. After two hours, Jeremiah was ahead by eight dollars. He had won a few hands and lost fewer but figured it was time to move on to a different table, which offered higher stakes.

By midnight, thanks to a drunken drummer's foolish bets, Jeremiah was over $100 ahead. When the opportunity came, he called it a night, bought a bottle of Kentucky whiskey and retired to his room. He poured a glass full then reflected on his new-found wealth. He had made enough money at the tables tonight to pay all of his expenses since arriving at the hotel and then some. No wonder Finimin had spent so much time and effort at the tables; he must have come out a big winner at some game in the distant past that had hooked him into wishful thinking.

Jeremiah gave thought to becoming a professional gambler, but he somehow knew that if he allowed himself to fall into any of the same pitfalls that George Finimin had, then the results could be disastrous. Gambling could be a helpful sideline in his travels, but he also needed something to fall back on when things became tight and he held no plans to abandon what he knew best. The potion sales gave him the perfect disguise to move about the country while looking for Emil Croft and possibly present another opportunity to cash in on capturing another wanted man. Being able to play cards for profit might even be helpful as well.

CHAPTER 9

The next morning, the visit he paid to the St Louis marshal's office was anything but cordial. When Jeremiah told Marshal Randall Brooks, a beefy middle-aged man with a round face and gray-streaked thinning hair, of his intentions, the man scowled. 'Bounty hunting is a damned sorry ass way to make a living, Hackett. What bounty hunters I know of are nothing more than murderous back-shooters. They live like rats and are no better grade than those they bring in. There are folks that say hunting a man for money is just as criminal as the thieves' and murderers' misdeeds. It can be dangerous as hell as well. Most of those on the run would gladly shoot you before they'd let you take them in.' He paused for a moment. 'Look,' he said in seeming exasperation, 'You are a clean-looking young man and look to me to be getting by OK by selling your stuff. Why don't you just stick with doing what you know best and leave the capturing of criminals to the law?'

Before Jeremiah could give an answer, the marshal gave his further opinion. 'You don't look so tough to me and why, hell, you aren't even carrying a six-gun. How are you going to get someone to give themselves up?'

'I have a shotgun that I keep in my carriage,' Jeremiah replied. He went on to tell Marshal Brooks about how he

58

had corralled the two train robbers without firing a shot.

Brooks shook his head back and forth in surprise, 'Sounds like what you pulled off was a fluke, a one-time happening that isn't likely to be repeated. You were lucky that things did not go sour. One of those men could have easily shot you full of holes. I still think it would be best if you would get this bounty hunting notion out of your head and go back to selling your potions.'

'Marshal, I have no intention of confronting anyone in a gun duel. As you pointed out, I would only get myself shot full of holes. All I am attempting is to familiarize myself with posters of men wanted by the law. That way I would at least know who they are.'

When Jeremiah asked a second time to see the wanted posters, Brooks shrugged his shoulders in disgust then pointed to a stack of the posters on a nearby second desk, 'You can take a look in that pile, a few local petty thieves named. They don't have much of a reward offered on them, maybe fifty dollars. You would most likely spend a month tracking down one of them and for fifty dollars, it would not be worth it. Any big reward money offered is out west where there isn't much law. And if you were to confront one of those mean bastards, you might end up getting shot for your trouble.'

In dismissal, the marshal then turned his attention to a paper he had been studying before Jeremiah's intrusion had disrupted his morning thoughts.

Jeremiah thumbed through the posters, but it was as Marshal Brooks had indicated; there were only listings for petty thieves with very little offered as a reward. A stipulation on one poster read that the reward offered was for the arrest and conviction of said person for the crime charged. That meant that even if he brought the person in, he would have to wait for a conviction before receiving the reward money. Jeremiah thanked the marshal then left. He did not take any of the posters with him, deciding to check things out in a different area. If he had to travel out west to find worthwhile game, then that is what he would do. He had decided to head out west to search for Emil Croft anyway.

Jeremiah thought about what the marshal had said about his not having a six-gun, so he decided to pay a visit to a gunsmith shop on Columbus Street. A thin man with a balding head and wearing round spectacles on the end of his nose sat behind a counter at a workbench with the parts of a six-gun spread out on the bench. The man looked up when the door opened. 'Can I help you, mister?'

Jeremiah stepped to a glass-fronted counter that displayed numerous handguns. 'I would like to look at your side arms,' he said, then cast his eyes to the six-guns on display. The gunsmith stood, then stepped three paces to the counter. 'I can most likely provide what you are looking for if I know a few particulars. Are you looking for a target pistol or one for personal protection? In other words, what are you going to do with it?'

Jeremiah brought his eyes up to meet the gunsmith's, 'I'd say it would be for personal protection. I travel around the country in my carriage and sell a few things. I have a double-barrel shotgun that I keep in the carriage, but I believe that a six-gun on my person might be a good idea. I am heading out west.'

The gunsmith bobbed his head, 'Take a look at those on the counter.'

Jeremiah looked at near a dozen handguns, some new, some used. He picked up one then another. All of the big bore .44 and .45 caliber six-guns felt heavy and cumbersome in his hand.

'You got anything not quite so heavy?' Jeremiah asked.

The gunsmith bobbed his head then went to a different counter and returned with a slightly smaller six-gun, which he handed to his potential customer. 'Try this one. It is an 1877 Colt Lightning. As you can tell, it is not as heavy as those other guns, but still packs a wallop. It takes a little lighter load in a .38 caliber. This particular model has a 7½ inch barrel and double action, meaning that you do not have to cock it to fire it, just pull the trigger. Let's step out back and you can take a few shots with it, see how it feels.' Jeremiah took the revolver in hand and he liked the feel of it.

Outside Jeremiah raised the weapon to eye level then fired shot after shot, all six shots at a bull's eye target, but none of them hit it. The gunsmith wagged his head in wonder, 'You ever had cause to use a six-gun before?'

Jeremiah shook his head, 'I never had a need to, but things have changed recently and I want to be ready.'

The gunsmith took the Colt from Jeremiah's hand and reloaded it. Showing great patience as if instructing a child, he began giving an oratory of how to hold the weapon, how to sight the target, to squeeze the trigger rather than pull it. 'Look the way you are shooting or you'll never hit anything. I have done quite a bit of shooting over the years. You have to treat the barrel of your six-gun like the extension of your finger. Point it and fire without all that aiming. Here, I'll show you.'

He turned facing the target area littered with cans on the ground. He fired from the hip. His first shot spun a can around. He followed up by making the can jump with the remaining shots. He finished by saying, 'All you need is some practice.'

A half hour later, Jeremiah left the gun shop with his new purchase, the Colt Lightning, a cross-draw holster fitted to his left hip that put the six-gun canted to the right across his stomach. By the gunsmith's recommendation, he also bought six boxes of .38 cartridges, intending to practice after making his daily camp.

Jeremiah, with new-found purpose in mind, was very careful in restocking his potion carriage. Things were different now. With money in his pocket, he felt no need to continue driving onto a farm to sell ten-cent items, then giving away penny candy to kids just to get a meal. He would skirt those places unless a need called for a visit. He opted to plan his travel so that he could take full advantage of eating and drinking at places along the way. Sure, that would limit his sales but a wanted man was not apt to be hiding out on a desolate farm anyway. He figured it would take some time and study of circulars in various areas before he could consider how to go about capturing a wanted man without getting himself killed. The reward price was a factor. If he were to be successful in this venture, then he would not waste his time going after a fifty-dollar chicken thief; $250 to $300 seemed like the least figure he would consider. It made sense as well to limit his time in the larger cities where an abundance of officers walked the streets. He would need to frequent out-of-the-way saloons and gambling places, which were the logical places a wanted man would most likely frequent.

CHAPTER 10

The next day he began his travel west. The main road leading west was dotted with plenty of small towns along the way, which allowed him to make enough potion sales to sustain himself and Chelsea's needs. He stayed in hotels and ate restaurant food. A week later, he turned south and decided to visit Sedalia. He had never visited the town before but remembered that Ryan and Basham had said that was where they had been the night they came into his camp. Maybe others of their ilk would be there, he reasoned.

He stayed for two nights while taking his time to look things over. He was able to make some potion sales during the day and enjoyed some small stakes poker games at night, but neither the potion sales nor the gambling proved very profitable. He learned nothing about any wanted men plaguing the town or the area. There were officers walking the streets, making a show of visiting the saloons frequently and the town was quiet. Jeremiah left the next morning, taking two days to reach Independence.

He spent the next four days making good potion sales to many going-to and coming-from travelers. Studying

wanted posters and night time visits to the saloons provided no positive leads on wanted men. From what he
could determine, it was just as Marshal Brooks had said
back in St Louis; all the bad hombres with a price on their
head were further out west where there was little or no law.
Perhaps Emil Croft was one of them.

Jeremiah spent the next two nights on the trail and was
able to get in some six-gun practice shooting at targets fifty
yards away. The first day and a full box of shells later did
nothing to improve his aim. The second day's early camp
and shooting practice, after adjustments, made a significant improvement in his shooting. He had gone through
half a box of shells before he moved the target closer to
about thirty yards. In the shortened distance things seem
to improve so he set the targets closer at twenty yards and
after a dozen shots was able to point, shoot and hit the
target or very near it at will. He found that by concentrating on the target rather than the muzzle of his six-gun that
he could pull the weapon then do as the gunsmith had
instructed by allowing the muzzle of the gun to be an
extension of his finger and pull the trigger. He finished
the shooting practice by pulling the fully loaded six-gun
from his holster and was able to bounce a can twice along
with four near misses. His confidence of handling the six-
gun soared. He was satisfied that in due time his abilities
with the six-gun would get better and he could then begin
to move the targets back a little. He reminded himself to
stock up on more bullets at the next opportunity.

A week later found him in Ellsworth, Kansas. In his estimation, this was a real cow town, with plenty of
rough-looking men on the streets. During the hours of
daylight, the town was no different from other towns he
had visited prior to arriving here. The cowboys riding into
town paid little to no attention to the wares he offered for

sale; it seemed they were more interested in getting inside a saloon. He had better luck with what town folk or visitors coming and going stopped by his carriage. A few folks bought some bottles of his mixtures before heading off to one of the various restaurants or shopping for necessities from the stores.

In the late afternoon when the business owners began to put out the closed signs, the saloons began to fill up. These saloons proved different from the subdued ones Jeremiah had frequented in the east where he came from. Jeremiah stepped into the Trail's End saloon, which was busy but not overly so, and made his way to the bar. He ordered a beer then stood back to survey the room.

There were three tables with poker games going on and all the chairs filled with eager players. When three cowboys vacated their seats, and stomped away from a table in the corner, Jeremiah walked over to stand behind one of the chairs. The dealer, a thin man wearing sleeve garters, a brocade vest, heavily pomaded hair and a perpetual smile looked up when Jeremiah put his hand on the chair back, 'Welcome stranger. Your money's good here.'

Two other men wearing cheap broadcloth suits sat across from the dealer. They both nodded when Jeremiah took a seat.

One of the men grinned, 'Yeah, the money is good in his pocket, if you aren't careful.'

The dealer did not respond but said, 'Twenty-five cent ante for five-card draw.'

All three bettors each threw a coin onto the center of the table.

Jeremiah did not intend to get drunk or get into any heavy gambling; he was here to observe and to listen to some local banter. He was in hope of learning of the activities of any wanted men.

Shortly after Jeremiah's arrival at the saloon, others began to filter in. They were clerks in shirtsleeves and business owners in broadcloth suits who took seats at tables, having come in for a drink after their day of labor. A drink or so and they began to drift away, replaced by a more boisterous crowd; men in rough-looking range wear, jingling spurs on their booted feet and a six-gun strapped to a hip. They were loud and profane, gabbing while swigging beer and downing shots of whiskey. Some lit big stinking cigars, clouds of smoke wreathing their heads, while others spat tobacco juice at spittoons and often missed. Hell, Jeremiah thought, almost every one of the loud, swaggering cowboys looked like criminals. The scattering of tables soon filled up, leaving others to crowd in to stand before the bar for their drinks. Others took seats at the gaming tables as chairs emptied. Two young cowboys with a drink in one hand and folding money in the other, seemingly eager to get some betting done, seated themselves in the two empty chairs at Jeremiah's table.

'Twenty-five cent antes, gentlemen, I'm your host, Joe Torres, and may I ask your names?' the dealer said.

Both cowboys threw a quarter into the pot, 'Joe Tiger,' one man said.

'Willie Schultz, we're just in from Fort Worth, Texas,' the other announced and grinned confidently, 'And we're ready to do some winning.'

The dealer smiled, 'Let's see what the cards reveal.' The suited man to Jeremiah's right introduced himself, 'I'm Fred Kinsey. I came in on the train this afternoon. I will be heading to Hays City in the morning. I sell general merchandise to dry goods stores.'

The other suited man nodded, 'I'm George Lang, I'm on the same train. Fred and I often travel together and sometimes we compete for customers but I sell clothing only.'

Jeremiah nodded then announced, 'Jeremiah Hackett. I am a stranger in these parts. I am a potion peddler by trade, just traveling by carriage into new territory. I figured to travel to Hays City then travel up north.'

'If you are headed out to that country west of here, be careful, my friend,' Fred said. 'Lots of road agents out that way. That is why George and I took to train travel. The last time we came by stage. About thirty miles further on west two masked robbers stopped the stage and shot the driver. The bastards took our watches and wallets. We stopped in to see the marshal in Hays City but all he did was to shake his head. He said there was not much he could do about it. He said it was out of his jurisdiction, but would let the Ellis county sheriff know. I could live with the money loss, but felt lucky to get out alive. Both of us swore off travel-ing this danger-filled land by any way other than by train. If you're set on making that trip, you might consider teaming up with some freighters or the stage.'

Jeremiah nodded, 'Thanks for the information, I'll be extra vigilant.'

Before long, a fight broke out at one of the other poker tables. A drunken cowboy jumped to his feet and accused the dealer of cheating. The cowboy ended up unconscious on the floor after the dealer hit him over the head with a hardwood club that he kept beside his chair. Within five minutes, two deputy marshals came rushing in. Apparently, the bartender had sent a messenger to summon them. The deputies questioned the bartender then the dealer. When satisfied that the drunken man caused the disturbance, each deputy took a hand under one of the cowboy's arms, dragged him upright then hauled him away. By ten o'clock Jeremiah decided to call it a night. He was eight dollars ahead, thanks to some wild betting by the cowboys, who had attempted to buy some pots but were steadily losing to superior players with better hands.

After Jeremiah went to bed, he heard several gunshots echoing in the night air. The gunshots gave him no cause for concern, figuring most likely that some over-exuberant cowboys was letting off steam by shooting at signs or such.

The next morning, he paid a visit to the marshal's office to find a deputy seated at a desk. The badge on the deputy's shirt did not seem appropriate on the thin, youthful-looking man. He had a smile on his blemish-free face and peach fuzz above his lip. 'Morning, sir, I'm Deputy Marshal Rich Alston, what I can do for you?' he asked as Jeremiah stepped inside and closed the door.

'Jeremiah Hackett, I'm just a traveler looking for some information,' Jeremiah replied. He did not want to say he was a bounty hunter and listen to any further reprimanding rhetoric, so he went under the guise of just being a traveler concerned about the robberies he had heard about along the road to Hays City where he intended to go.

The deputy twisted his mouth in a grimace then said, 'Marshal Johnson would most likely say that it is not a good idea to go off alone, mister, even in the daylight. Trouble is most apt to find you without warning. Why just two weeks ago, a traveler found a freight hauler shot dead and left alongside the road. The killers had taken everything the man owned, his mules, wagon and whatever he was hauling. There has been a lot of thieving west and north of Ellsworth and a number of posses have been out looking, but whoever is doing the hold-ups is damned slick. Some say it is the work of two well-known bandits. Others say it's the work of a whole gang.'

Jeremiah nodded, 'What are your thoughts on who is doing the dirty deeds, deputy?'

The deputy squeezed one eye to a squint when he looked at Jeremiah, 'Well personally, I think it's the work of Lenny Childers and Ben Atwood. Lenny grew up just north of here, so he knows the country. They say that when Childers was only fourteen he damned near beat his neighbor to death with a shovel. The neighboring man had caught him stealing watermelons. When collared, Lenny stabbed him with a knife then began beating him with the shovel. The man almost bled out right there in the field, but the man's wife came looking for him and was able to save him. Lenny left the country for a long time, some eight to ten years ago, and joined up with a gang, robbing stages, freighters and such all over the place. That went on for three or four years, then one day he took a bullet during a hold-up, knocked right off his horse. The rest of the gang left him. The people he was robbing brought him into town and a doctor saved his life. Soon after, there was a trial and he went to prison. About a year or so ago, he and Ben Atwood broke out of the prison cell they shared and now the pair of them are back raising all kinds of hell. Atwood is just as cold-blooded, known to kill a man for his valuables without hesitation. Fact is, both those owl hoots have papers on them and they don't dare to show their faces here or any other place that has lawmen working the streets.'

'Do you mind if I look at those posters, deputy? If I happen to see them, I want to be as ready as I can be.'

The deputy pointed to a stack of posters sitting on the corner of the desk. 'Go ahead and have a look-see. You'll find them in there. The reward is a thousand dollars per man, dead or alive, but I don't think that any lawmen are hot on their trail; not even any bounty hunters are after them that I know of.'

Jeremiah looked through the stack, mentally noting fliers on other criminals, but the posters looked old; the men whose descriptions were on them had most likely moved on to different locales and taken to using different names. When he found the two papers that gave the descriptions of Childers and Atwood, he asked, 'Mind if I take these along with me, deputy?'

The deputy shrugged. 'Sure, go ahead, I've got a whole stack of them. Been aiming to tack some up around town for all the good it would do.'

Jeremiah thanked the deputy then went to the livery, paid his bill, hitched Chelsea up to the carriage and left town.

The liveryman advised him that the shortest way to Hays City was to take the road west for about twenty miles. The road ran right alongside the Smoky River to the Saline River.

'When you come to a small lake, you will be at the junction to the well-traveled road to Hays City. From the junction, Hays City is another thirty-five or forty miles,' the man said. He then went on to say that there were some small farming community towns along the way, but was not sure what accommodation they might offer. Road agents or not, Jeremiah figured he would travel until near dark then make a camp, just as he and Chelsea had done many times in the past.

CHAPTER 11

When Jeremiah had traveled for around five hours, he spotted what looked like the roof of a building off in the distance, situated near the shore of a lake or possibly just the widening of the Saline River. He spotted some movement in front of the structure. He pulled Chelsea to a halt then reached under the seat for his expanding telescope. He put the telescope to his eye and watched curiously, as two mounted men began riding their horses away. The riders were tugging along two saddled but riderless mounts behind them. Jeremiah watched until the riders had disappeared down the road to the west.

At least the liveryman back in Ellsworth had been right in his estimation and Jeremiah figured that he had traveled about twenty miles since leaving the town. As he drove the carriage closer, he could see the road that the liveryman spoke of running east/west a stone's throw from the building he had spotted. He decided to drive over to the building and let Chelsea water at the lake and rest for an hour or so before traveling on. The building was weathered gray, ravaged by time and neglect. A door in the front wall of the old building was open. Off to the right was what was left of an empty corral, many of the poles of the surround were leaning and one post had fallen over. The place did not look like a homestead. It was most likely an old stage relay station but was obviously abandoned, perhaps a victim of the coming of the railroad.

Jeremiah drove the carriage to stop in front of the building. He stepped down from the carriage and decided to look inside just to satisfy his curiosity. He stepped through the door. The place was just a dirt-floored hovel, rife with the sour gamey stench of wild critters and mouse droppings. No one had occupied this place recently, perhaps not for years.

He went ahead and unhitched Chelsea from the carriage and attached a lead rope, then led her to go around the building. He was set to lead the mule over to the lake for water. When he stepped alongside the building to the back, what he saw made his heart give a leap. Chelsea balked, pulling back on the lead rope after gaining a scent. Some twenty feet away toward the lake, a man was lying on his stomach. The back of the man's shirt was colored scarlet and he had a fist-sized hole in the middle of his back. Jeremiah reached to place a hand on his holstered .38.

He drew his six-gun, then let his eyes sweep around but nothing moved anywhere. Apparently, the killer was no longer around. He holstered the .38, then tied Chelsea's lead rope to a straggly bush and ran a hand down her neck to calm the animal. He then stepped warily to stand over the obviously dead man. A blackened swarm of flies rose as he waved an arm over the body. It looked as if the man may have been running away when a load of buckshot from a shotgun caught up with him.

The grizzly remains brought bile to Jeremiah's mouth.

The memory of the sickening sight of George Finimin killed in a similar fashion flashed in his mind. He quickly put a handkerchief to his mouth to suppress a rising gorge. A blast from a shotgun did terrible damage to the human body. The shot pellets in the load not only put a large hole in a body but also carried away great chunks of flesh and innards. He looked away to compose himself for a moment, then turned to look at the body again. At least the man had died quickly. By closer inspection of the corpse, Jeremiah could see that the man had a smaller hole, perhaps the size of a pistol shot in the back of his head. Whoever had killed the man certainly wanted him dead. They had shot him in the back with a shotgun to put him down then walked up and shot him in the back of the head where he lay. A spray of dried blood and bone matter had fanned out around the man's head.

Jeremiah figured that he would take a closer look around, in case he might find other victims lying nearby. He went ahead and led Chelsea to the lake shore and hobbled her then retraced his steps to go on a search. He stood holding his hand above his eyes to shield out the sun and give a full search all around but spotted nothing. There was scarcely any vegetation other than browned grass up to the lakeshore where there was some green and a few scruffy looking bushes, but not enough cover to conceal anyone. He went back to the front of the building in hopes he could find some of the man's belongings or at least something to cover the body. What he found was nothing. The only place he had not looked was inside what was left of the small, dilapidated barn next to the corral. One wall had collapsed outward, which caused the edge of the roof to cant sharply toward the ground.

He spent a few minutes looking the place over and determined that it held nothing of interest. The killer was long gone. He went back to the body and turned the man over. The man, light of weight and slim, possibly forty years old, had blue eyes frozen in a death stare. Jeremiah bent to kneel on one knee beside the body and began a search of the man's pockets in hopes of finding an identity. He was concentrating on the search, then was suddenly startled by a movement behind him.

Jeremiah instantly reached for his six-gun, then dived to his right to roll on his shoulder. He had the six-gun out and trained on the intruder by the time he completed the defensive maneuver. He was on his back and had the six-gun pointed and ready to fire, but held off when the person came into view. A thin youngster in his mid-teens, Jeremiah judged, and noted that he was shivering from the light breeze blowing. He was soaking wet and had obviously just came from the lake.

Jeremiah swept his eyes around to see if there were others, but the only movement was Chelsea cropping grass by the lakeshore. He stood to face the tall skinny kid, with a sunburned hawkish face; his brown hair plastered to his head by the water. Jeremiah took note that the young man was barefoot, his feet white and shriveled from too much time in the water.

Jeremiah, satisfied that the kid was no threat, holstered his six-gun. 'Who are you? What are you doing here?'

The kid swallowed then squinted his eyes, 'I, uh. . . .'

He paused then lifted a hand toward the body. Jeremiah could see that the young man was most likely suffering from shock and in need of some quiet time before he would be able to talk coherently.

'It's OK. You are safe now. I will not harm you,' Jeremiah soothed. 'Was this man a relative, your father?'

The kid shook his head side to side.

'But you knew him?'

The kid nodded.

'Come with me around front to my carriage. I'll give you something to drink and you can dry off.'

Jeremiah stepped away; he could hear the soft footsteps of the kid following. At the carriage, Jeremiah lifted one hinged side to prop open with a stick. He took a towel in hand and a container of bag balm then held them out to the youngster.

'Why don't you dry off then sit down and smear some of this balm on your feet; it will help. I have a spare pair of socks you can have.' The kid, with eyes wide, hesitated then took the towel and wiped his face and hair. He sat down on the ground and began spreading the balm over his galled feet. Jeremiah handed him a bottle of Finimin's Golden Elixir, figuring the alcohol in the mixture might help revive the youth.

Jeremiah reached underneath the carriage and unhooked a shovel. He then turned to face the still seated young man who was now sipping the Golden Elixir. 'We need to give that man a decent burial before some scavengers come prowling.' The kid nodded and began pulling on the socks Jeremiah had given him then he stood.

Jeremiah led the way back to the body.

The late afternoon sun was moving closer to the western horizon by the time Jeremiah and the kid had finished burying the man on a spot near the lakeshore. The youth stood silently with his eyes cast on the grave as Jeremiah smoothed out the last of the dirt. The youngster seemed reluctant to step away. Jeremiah knew how the kid felt, having previously experienced the loss of his friend and mentor George Finimin in a similar fashion. He tossed the shovel away then stepped to stand beside the young man and took his hat off. 'If you want me to say a

75

word or so over this man then I need to know his name,' Jeremiah stated.

'Mister Ticker,' he said in a soft voice. It was the first words the kid had said.

Jeremiah nodded then cleared his throat, 'This man Mister Ticker was a good man, who was shot dead for unknown reason. We ask that he rest in peace and that his killer be brought to justice for taking this man's life.' Jeremiah paused for a moment then said, 'Amen.'

With that, he turned away and picked up the shovel then began walking toward Chelsea.

The young man began walking along beside him.

Jeremiah kept stepping along and knew the young man was at a loss as to what to do next. He figured to give the youngster some direction.

'Let's get Chelsea in the harness and get on down the road a piece, then we can make a camp for the night. I will wager that you are as hungry as I am. I have some canned peaches that ought to taste good. We can talk things out around a campfire. I am on my way to Hays City. You might just as well ride along with me. When we get there, you can report to the sheriff what happened here. Maybe the sheriff can locate and arrest whoever did this. The sheriff would most likely help you to contact your relatives. I would wager they would be happy to know that you are all right. How does that sound?'

The kid shook his head side to side. 'I'll go as far as Hays City, but I'm not going back to Kansas City,' he said defiantly.

Jeremiah did not want to push the issue but figured to get the kid to talk some. 'My name is Jeremiah Hackett. What is your name?'

'Lester Cummings.'

'Well, Lester, let's go find a campsite away from here.'

Lester nodded. They both lined Chelsea up and when ready they climbed onto the carriage and seated themselves.

CHAPTER 12

A half an hour later, Jeremiah Hackett could plainly see in the distance ahead the two galloping riders leading two saddled horses down the road toward the carriage. The riders were a way off yet, but the horses were kicking up a column of dust as they hurried along. Lester, seated next to Jeremiah, suddenly grabbed Jeremiah's arm while pointing a hand toward the riders.

'That's them!' he exclaimed. 'Those are the dirty sonsofbitches that killed Ticker and took our horses!'

Jeremiah pulled the lines leading to his little mule to stop the box carriage. 'Crawl in the back and stay quiet. We'll wait here and I'll see of their business.'

'But they might shoot you too,' the young man argued.

'I can handle it,' Jeremiah assured him, though his heart was thumping wildly. 'You just get in the back and stay out of sight like I said to do.'

The young man did as told and slipped behind the seat through a black canvas curtain. Jeremiah pulled his six-gun from his cross-draw holster, careful to hold it out of site just below the lip of the raised fronting of the carriage, which was knee height before him.

When the two riders neared to within fifty yards they

slowed their horses to a walk, causing their kicked-up dust cloud to close around them as they approached. One man held a lead rope trailing the riderless horses; the other moved a few feet to one side. Neither man had pulled their six-guns but each man had a hand on or near the handle of a six-gun on their side.

The one holding the lead rope pulled his horse to stop almost nose to nose with Chelsea. Jeremiah figured that the man was about thirty years old. He was a sunburned, hard-looking man, his clothes dusty and wrinkled with wear. Jeremiah sat stolidly as the man dropped the lead ropes of the two unsaddled horses then pulled a bandanna to mop over his face and neck. He then lifted his hat exposing a slicked down mop of dark curly hair. He wiped the inside of the hat before replacing on his head.

'It gets a might hot out here this time of day,' he said matter-of-factly as if talking to a neighborhood friend.

Jeremiah instinctively knew this was a dangerous situation. He did not say anything but merely glared at the man, studying him, wary of any sudden movement. He recognized Lenny Childers' face as the one depicted on the wanted poster he had studied, a copy of which he had in the carriage. The man was wanted for murder and robbery, and had a thousand dollars, dead or alive, on his head, according to the poster. Jeremiah's heart thumped even more wildly. The other rider was most likely Childers' partner in crime, Ben Atwood. He was worth a thousand dollars as well. The confrontation had happened just as the deputy back in Ellsworth had said, without warning.

Strangely, Jeremiah was not afraid, but wary. He was alert, his nerves steeled to what would happen next. This was exactly the reason he had come to this part of the country; to locate Emil Croft was the priority, but if he could take crooks like Childers and Atwood in for the bounty on their heads, so much the better. They were bad men trying to make a mark on the world, but bad men nearly always fail in the end. They just could not escape from the grim nemesis that beckons from the grave to the criminal to step forward to a violent end. Jeremiah's mind was active while watching every move the man made.

Childers retied the bandanna around his neck then let his right hand slowly drop to the handle of his holstered six-gun in a way that seemed as if it were a natural thing to do, but Jeremiah had noted his movement. Childers straightened in the saddle, then glared sullenly at Jeremiah.

'What are you doing out here, mister? Didn't anyone tell you that it is risky to travel along this stretch of road?'

Jeremiah nodded, 'I was told.'

Childers grinned, 'And you ignored that advice and came anyway, figuring no bad guys would take notice of you traveling along. Well let me tell you, you ain't dealing with no green first-timers and there is a price for you traveling through our territory. Nothing gets past us, out here on the road. I have a good telescope and I've been watching you. I saw when the kid showed up and the two of you buried that guy.'

Jeremiah nodded, 'He needed some help.' He paused a moment, 'Now it comes to what do you want with either of us?'

Childers grinned and cackled, 'Did you hear that, Ben? He wants to know what we stopped him for.' He then glared back at Jeremiah. 'We're gonna take everything, mister – the mule, the carriage and all. If you don't agree to it, then we'll just shoot you. You and the kid have one chance. Take off right now and start walking back to Ellsworth before I change my mind.'

He jerked his head toward Ben, an older man, who was

ten feet away, 'Go around back and get that kid out of the carriage.'

Ben slid off his horse then stepped alongside the carriage.

Neither man had drawn his six-gun yet; perhaps, by their arrogance, they figured that the carriage travelers were no threat. Jeremiah had his six-gun out of sight and in his hand, knowing he would have to do something, but wondering when to make his move. He could for sure shoot one of them but facing two gunmen was a bit taxing. He tensed as Ben passed by him. He could have easily shot the man and would have had Ben gotten close enough to see the gun in his hand. At this point, Jeremiah figured to wait until Ben was busy harassing the kid before making his move on Childers and then take care of Ben. Jeremiah was ready.

Childers apparently forgot he had just ordered Jeremiah and the kid to take off walking. It appeared that he wanted to talk some more, 'What's your name, mister, and what are you doing here?'

'Hackett,' Jeremiah said, 'I'm on my way to Hays City. I sell potions and medicinal concoctions.'

Childers nodded, 'I seen some lettering on the carriage. Well, Doc Hackett, it's the end of the line for you. Now step down from that carriage.'

Ben Atwood had rounded the corner of the carriage out of site. He then reached a hand out to pull aside the black canvas curtain that covered the back of the carriage. When he pulled the curtain to one side, a deafening blast of a shotgun fired from inside the carriage met him. The twelve-gauge load hit the man in the middle of his chest, propelling him several feet backwards to land on his back, his legs quivering and he was quite dead.

The sudden noise of the shotgun blast rattled the carriage and startled both Jeremiah and Childers. Chelsea, unaccustomed to the loud noise, danced in the traces, whereas Childers' horse did not even flinch. Childers immediately streaked a hand to his six-gun. Childers had managed to pull his six-gun out of the holster, and was attempting to swing the muzzle up, when his motion abruptly stopped. Two bullets from Jeremiah's six-gun to Childers' heart caused the gunman to pull the trigger sending one erratic shot off to nowhere, some five feet off target. Childers' body was flung back by the impact of the bullets, his feet coming free of the stirrups. He then fell over the rump of his horse, causing the horse to buck and kick out his back hoofs, then dance away. Childers's body now lay in the dusty road, twitching as blood poured from the two holes in his chest.

Jeremiah knew Childers was out of it, but wondered about Atwood. The shotgun blast meant something went on back there. He wondered what had transpired behind him. Jeremiah dived to the ground then went into a crouch with his six-gun extended in a defensive maneuver. He edged toward the back of the carriage, ready to react if need be.

Jeremiah flinched when the kid unexpectedly stepped from behind the carriage. Jeremiah swallowed hard. He had almost pulled the trigger on his six-gun. The kid had Jeremiah's twelve-gauge double-barreled shotgun. Smoke was still curling out of the right barrel.

'I shot that bastard just like he shot Ticker. I still got one barrel left that I was hoping to let loose on that other one,' he said excitedly with his eyes flaring.

Jeremiah put a hand, palm out to stop the youth. 'He's been taken care of. It's over for now, but let's take a look at both of them to make sure.'

Jeremiah stood up then stepped around to view the body of Ben Atwood. He then led the way for the two to stand over the body of Lenny Childers, 'Looks to me like they are both done for.'

He placed a hand to the kid's shoulder, 'You did good. No telling what would have happened if they had their way and things went any further.'

He then plucked the shotgun from the youth's hands, let the hammer down and laid it next to the carriage seat. 'Why don't you go gather up all those horses before they scatter further. We'll need to load these bodies up and take them to the law in Hays City.'

Lester gave him a look of wonder. 'Why don't we just leave them for the buzzards?' he exclaimed, 'That's the way they left Ticker.'

Jeremiah motioned with his hand toward the carriage, 'You've got a point, but let me show you something.' He raised a hinged side of the carriage then placed a stick to hold it up. He then fished into a slot and produced the two Wanted posters with Lenny Childers and Ben Atwood's likenesses showing. He stuck them out toward the kid, 'Go take a look at their faces. They are worth a thousand dollars apiece if the bodies are turned in to the authorities.'

The kid looked at the posters and smiled. 'You really think so? You think they would give us the money if we brought them in?'

Jeremiah nodded, 'That's what the posters say. When we turn them in, a thousand dollars goes to you for shooting Atwood and a thousand dollars to me for shooting Childers. In addition, we can take their weapons if we want and you get your and your friend's horses back. Check the saddle-bags for your boots.'

Lester stood with eyes wide, 'They won't pay any bounty to me. Everyone in town knows me for just being a kid.'

Jeremiah grinned, 'That poster doesn't look to me like

it has an age limit on it, but if you are worried about it, then I'll collect for both of them and split with you later.'

Lester nodded.

Jeremiah and the kid worked together searching the bodies for valuables. Both men had their spending money, a small amount of cash, inside a shirt pocket, which together amounted to $42. Jeremiah counted out $21 and handed it to Lester.

'I believe that we are entitled to their pocket cash,' Jeremiah said. Jeremiah found a two-shot .41-caliber der-ringer in one of Childers' boots, which he stuck into his own pocket. He and Lester then searched the saddlebags, finding numerous items of stolen jewelry, money clips and watches.

'We'll turn this stuff into the law,' Jeremiah said. 'Maybe someone can identify some of it and most likely be happy to get it back.'

When done, they rolled each of the bloody bodies into the outlaws' own blankets carried behind their saddles. They loaded each of the bodies onto the outlaws' horses then tied the reins to the back of the carriage. When they started off, Jeremiah had Chelsea lead off while Lester rode his own reclaimed horse alongside the carriage. He held a lead rope to Ticker's horse that easily followed along.

An hour later, they made a camp in a copse of cotton-wood trees beside a trickling creek. They unloaded the bodies to lie beside the carriage then Lester unsaddled the horses and hobbled each of them while Jeremiah scav-enged enough dead brush and sticks to make a fire and set coffee on to boil. It was already November and the night would be cold.

After a meal of fried potatoes, bacon, bread and coffee and canned peaches for dessert, the two travelers lounged near the campfire.

Lester must have figured it time to tell of his past. 'I told you earlier that my name is Lester Cummings. Now I will tell you how I come to be here. The man we buried is Mr Ticker, my friend. He worked for my grandmother. I think his first name was Melvin, but my grandmother insisted I refer to him as Mr Ticker. I watched those men kill him, shot him down like a stray dog. I do not know why they shot him. We weren't bothering anyone. I was in the lake cooling off when I heard a shout. I looked over to that shack, where we were planning to camp for the rest of the day, and saw Ticker running toward the lake. I saw the tall one, the one with the cowhide vest, following behind Ticker. He raised a shotgun up then shot Ticker in the back. The other one walked up and stood over Ticker then shot him again with his pistol.

'They must have known that I was around somewhere because they spent a good deal of time calling out to me to come in, said it was OK, that they would not harm me, but I did not believe them. I figured they would kill me too. It was getting cold as heck but I stayed in the water. Both of them came down to edge of the lake and looked around. I figured they couldn't see me the way my body was under water and just the top of my head and eyes above the surface. I had swum under some long grass growing over the edge of the bank some twenty feet away from them. I could see them but they couldn't see me. I heard one of them say, "Hell, that kid is long gone. Let's get out of here." I heard the horses when they left. I looked out from my hiding place and watched them go. They took my horse and the one Ticker was riding, which was my dad's, and everything we had with us. Sonsofbitches even took my boots I'd left on the lake shore.' He raised a booted foot up to show that he had

85

retrieved them. 'It wasn't long after that I watched when you showed up.'

When Lester paused for a long moment, Jeremiah figured Lester was finished talking, then the youth began again.

'Four years ago, my pa moved my step-ma Lou Ann and me from Kansas City to a homestead near Hays City. Pa had studied things out before we ever came here. He said the area was a good place to grow Turkey Red Wheat. As it turned out though, it was a hard place to make a living. Lou Ann gave up about a year ago; she and Pa were not getting along very good anyway. She took the train back to Kansas City. Lou Ann never mentioned that I should go with her, and did not argue when Pa said he needed me on the farm. I don't believe that she liked me very well all along. Pa had married her a year or so after my mother died. He told me that when things got better he was going to send for Lou Ann to come back, but I did not believe that she would do that. Things never got any better; fact is, they got worse. We didn't get enough rain and the wheat crop dried up. I could tell Pa was mighty worried; he wouldn't eat much and never seemed to sleep. One day Pa took sick and stayed in bed. I wanted to go for a doctor but he told me no. "We don't have any money for that. I'll be OK in couple days," he said.

'After two days, I tried to wake him, but he only moaned and rolled over. I went into Hays City and found a doctor, but Pa had already died by the time we got back. The doctor helped me bury Pa then insisted that I go see Sheriff McDaniel. The sheriff said that he would get in touch with my step-ma and grandmother in Kansas City but I did not want to go back there; I told him that I now owned the homestead, just outside town and that I had things to see to there, animals and such, and that I could take care of myself. Mr Jacobs down at the livery told me he would see to my horse's eats if I would help doing the afternoon chores and that I could sleep in the tack room at night, to kind of keep watch over the place. He even provided me with food of a night. I would ride out to the homestead in the mornings and see to Dad's horse and such.

'I thought the arrangement was working out quite well, then one day Mr Ticker showed up off the train. I found out later that the sheriff had made a deal with Mr Jacobs to kind of look after me until my relatives sent someone to take me back to Kansas. Ticker told me the sheriff had sent my folks a telegram and my grandmother figured I was too young to make it on my own, so she sent Ticker out to fetch me back. Ticker wanted us to take the train, but I did not want to have to sell the horses, so I talked him into us riding back. Now I am sorry for that because it got him killed.'

Jeremiah nodded his head in understanding, 'Well, Lester, a lot of folks would like to turn the calendar back and do things different, but things are the way they are and we all have to just keep going.'

'How old are you?' Jeremiah asked.

Lester glared defiantly, 'I'll be sixteen next month.'

CHAPTER 13

It was mid-afternoon the following day when Lester, leading the way on his horse, and Jeremiah, driving the carriage with the two body-laden horses following close behind, made their way down the main street of Hays City. Folks on the boardwalks stopped to stare; some pointed a finger and mumbled questioningly to each other as the strange carriage and the two body-bearing horses passed by. Lester had gigged his horse to lead the way to the sheriff's office, with the carriage following. Lester guided his horse to a tie rail in front of the barred windows of the jail, hopped down and tied his reins, then pulled Ticker's horse in. Jeremiah brought Chelsea to a halt behind them.

A number of townsmen stepped hurriedly toward the jail, curious as to who the bodies were and how they had met their end.

When the door to the sheriff's office opened, a tall, middle-aged, suited man with a star on his vest front stepped out on the boardwalk. Sheriff Dag McDaniel lifted his hat with one hand then let it settle back on to his head as he stood in wonder. When Lester stepped forward, the sheriff asked, 'What are you doing back here, Lester? Where's your friend?'

Lester flared a hand toward the bodies on the horses, 'They killed him yesterday, so me and Mr Hackett killed them; brought 'em in for the reward.'

The sheriff, flabbergasted by what the youth had just said, was ready to ask more when Jeremiah stepped forward. He stuck out his hand, 'Howdy Sheriff, my name is Jeremiah Hackett.

The sheriff shook hands, 'Dag McDaniel, let's go into my office so you can tell me what's going on here before we get more of a crowd on hand.'

Lester opened the door and stepped inside, and then Jeremiah went in, followed by the sheriff. The sheriff closed the door then stepped to his desk and took a seat. Jeremiah and Lester took ladder-back chairs in front of the desk.

'OK, let's start from the beginning,' he directed to Jeremiah.

In a short time, Jeremiah had told of his arriving at the old stage stop then discovering the deceased man and Lester's arrival. Lester jumped in to retell how the two outlaws had killed Ticker and how he had hidden in the water. He went on to tell of seeing the killers leave a short time before Jeremiah arrived. He then told of the two of them burying Ticker.

Sheriff McDaniel nodded, 'Okay, now Lester stated earlier that the two of you killed those two men you have draped over the backs of those horses. Who are they?'

Jeremiah reached a hand to his jacket pocket and brought out the wanted posters on both men. He handed them across the desk to the sheriff. The sheriff took the posters and glared at each one. Before he could make a comment, the door suddenly swung open and a very excited fresh-faced young man with a badge on his shirt came scurrying in.

'Sheriff, that's Lenny Childers and Ben Atwood out there; they been shot and they're both dead!'

The sheriff with a tired expression on his face sighed, 'Thanks, Leonard, now I don't have to go look at them.'

The sheriff turned his attention back to Jeremiah, 'Tell me about it from the beginning, where you come from and what you are doing in this country?'

Jeremiah took a breath then related to the sheriff his witnessing George Finimin's death, which was the reason he had come to be on the road to Hays City in his quest to find Emil Croft.

The sheriff digested the information, then said, 'You say you were hunting for this other man, Emil Croft, when Lester and then later those two showed up. Are you a professional bounty hunter?'

He was disbelieving that this clean looking young man would hunt men for bounty.

Jeremiah shook his head slightly, 'Professionally, I am a potion salesman and came to this part of the country, as I told you, in an attempt to locate Emil Croft. So far, I have not struck his trail. In the meantime, when the opportunity presents itself, I have prepared myself to take full advantage of a situation such as taking on Childers and Atwood.'

The sheriff, obviously surprised by Jeremiah's answer, asked, 'Have you brought others in for the bounty offered on them?'

Jeremiah nodded, and then took the time to tell of his earlier capture of Bill Ryan and Tucker Basham.

The sheriff almost smiled, 'Sounds to me like you got lucky, and then with all that easy money at your disposal, you decided to go on a hunt for others?'

Jeremiah shook his head, 'Not full time, Sheriff. It is as I said earlier; my main goal is to hunt down Emil Croft. A little over a year ago, I witnessed him murder my partner, George Finimin, down in Arkansas. I learned from a good

90

source that Croft had a homestead at one time, some-where in north-western Kansas, and I have reason to believe that he may have returned to there. It is only of recent that I could afford to go on a serious hunt.'

Jeremiah paused then asked, 'Have you any knowledge of the whereabouts of Emil Croft?'

The sheriff shook his head from side to side, 'That name doesn't ring a bell, but you're welcome to look over the wanted posters.'

He paused then continued, 'So, while looking for this Croft fella, you just happen to stumble onto some bad guys who have a price on their head and things worked out for you to collect the bounties on them?'

'Actually, in both instances, they were the ones that came to me,' Jeremiah said. 'It's like I said before, I'm just a potion salesman.'

The sheriff cut him a hard glare. 'If I were you, I would not figure on your string of luck having any longevity. Now, let's get back to this business. What happened before you two shot Childers and Atwood; I mean why did you shoot them?'

Jeremiah shrugged, 'I recognized them for who they were from the posters I got from the marshal's office in Ellsworth. When we first spotted them, I had Lester crawl out of sight into the back of the carriage. They came to a stop in front of me, and then Childers sent his partner Atwood to fetch Lester from the back of the carriage. Childers then told me they intended to take my carriage; said he would shoot us if we did not just walk away. It was plain that they meant harm to Lester and me, so I didn't figure I owed him or his partner anything but a bullet.'

The sheriff nodded his understanding, 'Ben Atwood and Lenny Childers were rowdy no-accounts, killers who thought they could do anything they pleased and no one

91

could stand in their way and, up until now, they were right. Both were too slick for the law and too deadly for lesser-known bounty hunters to chance going after them. How is it you come to get the drop on them?'

Jeremiah pointed a thumb to Lester. 'Lester was the one witnessed the killing of his friend. Therefore, that gave him the right to shoot Atwood when the man was coming to drag him from his hidey-hole in the carriage. I'm glad that Lester did, otherwise they may have killed both of us.'

The sheriff nodded, 'And you say you recognized them both from the posters you had on them?'

'I got those posters from the marshal's office in Ellsworth,' Jeremiah said. 'I wasn't purposefully hunting them for the money. It just happened like Lester and I have said.'

The sheriff, clearly surprised by the explanation, sat back in his chair. 'Well from the law's standpoint, we are glad that you found them. There will not be any mourners at their burying. Those two are just two less rats to have to worry about. There have been quite a number of robberies attributed to those two. Did they have any amount of loot with them?'

Jeremiah acknowledged what he knew. 'You'll find that their saddle-bags contain some jewelry, rings, necklaces, watches and such, which I believe are stolen.'

McDaniel nodded, 'Figures that they would have already spent any ready cash and kept those other items for trading purposes. I will inventory them and make an effort to get any identifiable items back to their rightful owners – that is, if they are still alive. The horses, saddles and such will go to burying those two. You can make a bid for them, if you want to keep them.'

Jeremiah shook his head, 'I don't have a need for a

saddle horse, Sheriff, and Lester already has two of his own.'

McDaniel nodded. 'I'll sign a paper verifying their deaths so you can receive the rewards due. It might take a day or so for the authorization to arrive for the bank to make the payout. For Lester's sake, I would recommend that we put both rewards claim in your name alone, Hackett. The less people know of Lester's involvement, the better. We do not need him to gain any kind of reputation with a gun. You two can work it out among yourselves.'

He continued to face Jeremiah. 'Now here is something to think about. You and Lester bringing in Childers and Atwood is a big deal, news wise. Mortimer Ames, the editor over at the Hays City Centennial is going to want to know all about how you were able to get the drop on those two, deadly as they were. I do not think it would be a good idea to fess up to Lester taking out Atwood. It would be better for Lester's sake if you two fabricate a story to tell the man about how you alone got the drop on both of them. No sense in trying to dodge the newspaperman, ole Mort can be damn persistent when he is onto a story and all the folks witnessing you bringing those bodies in are going to want to know all about it. As it is, as soon as word gets out, do not be surprised if a want-a-be gunman calls on you. In their mind, the man who took Childers and Atwood down will have a reputation worthy of challenge. I would advise you to take that six-gun off that you have around your middle. If some stranger were to call you out, best to walk away and let me handle the situation. Doing what I say would ensure that your short stay in Hays City would be a safe and quiet one. Once you get the rewards, you'd be wise to leave town.'

Jeremiah nodded his understanding. 'Sheriff, I can

appreciate what you said, but the truth of it is, I do not have a quarrel with anyone other than the one man that I came to this country to settle with, which is Emil Croft. I have no intention of getting into a fast draw contest with anyone just for the sake of gaining a reputation.'

McDaniel took a breath. 'Well, those that make this kind of thing their business are bound to their habits. I have seen their kind before, young and brash, full of themselves. Easy enough to recognize the way they wear their Colt halfway to their knees. The stupid ones, who are convinced that no one can beat them in a fast draw, usually do not last past the second or third shootout. Atwood and Childers will join alongside a couple of them who lost their bid for fame, in a pasture next to the honorable folks' cemetery. I am just saying that you need to be on the lookout.

'If you hang around town very long and the word gets out, do not be surprised if a complete stranger calls you out. As I said earlier, you need to take off that six-gun while in town. My deputies run things tight out on the streets and will look out for you, if I tell them to.'

He then turned to Lester, 'Once you two divvy up the reward, why don't we book you on a train to Kansas City? It seems to me that would be the safest way for you to get on home.'

Lester shook his head, 'I didn't want to go back there to start with. I am a property owner and now that I have money coming in, I intend to stay here. It is my home and my grandmother can come out to visit me, if she wants to. Some of that money is going to pay the taxes on my place so that John Andrews over at the bank won't take it.' He cast a glance to Jeremiah. 'Jeremiah is welcome to come out to the place and stay as long as he wants to. That way he doesn't have to pay to stay in town and worry about

94

someone calling him out.'

Jeremiah turned to Dag McDaniel. 'That suit you, Sheriff?'

McDaniel eyed Jeremiah for a silent moment as he rolled things over in his mind. 'How old are you, Jeremiah?'

'On my last birthday I turned twenty-two, Sheriff,' Jeremiah said.

McDaniel nodded, 'Not that much older than Lester.' He then said, 'It isn't up to me to decide Lester's future. As the sheriff, it is my duty to look out for the wellbeing of everyone in the county, and that includes Lester. I can let Lester's grandmother know of his desire to stay on the farm. If you as a legal age say that you'll become his guardian until he's of age, and providing Lester's grandmother agrees that he can stay on his property, then I have no objection.'

Jeremiah was at first taken aback by this declaration. He had just now gotten here. He did not know anything about this part if the country or what to expect at Lester's place. For that matter, he did not know Lester that well. Jeremiah had struck out from his own home as a loner, then George Finimin had taken him on when he was a little older than Lester was. That fact alone helped him to make up his mind. Why not emulate Finimin, take on an assistant, and give Lester some direction. Lester had already proved to be a good traveling companion and he was a gutsy kid, that was for sure.

The proposed arrangement prompted Jeremiah to consider things. If he did agree to look out for Lester, then that fact alone could put a crimp in his quest to find Emil Croft, if his guardianship lasted for a lengthy time. Over a year had already passed by since Finimin's death and his having to wait a little longer to find the murderer did not seem to matter much. As far as he was concerned, a delay would not change the outcome he had planned once Croft was located. Staying here for a while just might work out, however, in that what time he would spend here would provide the opportunity to familiarize himself with the countryside and perhaps get a lead on Emil Croft's whereabouts.

Jeremiah nodded. 'Sheriff, I left home when I was Lester's age and managed to make it on my own without a guardian to look over my shoulder. Just how old do you think Lester will have to be before he can call his own shots?'

Sheriff McDaniel shrugged his shoulders. 'Depends on the circumstance, I reckon. Before, Lester was alone, flat broke and in need of direction. I figured it was best for all, at the time, that he went back to his folks. Since you and Lester brought those bodies in, things have changed. Once you receive the rewards, he will have money and a home to call his own. I believe it would cement the deal of him staying here, if a more mature person were to say they'd look out for him for a time.'

Without hesitation, Jeremiah nodded. 'OK, then I agree.'

McDaniel stood then said, 'Very well then, I'll let you know what his grandmother says about the arrangement. Check with me day after tomorrow. I might have heard from her by then. It will most likely take that much time to get authorization to pay out the bounties you and Lester have coming anyway.'

CHAPTER 14

When Jeremiah and Lester stepped outside the sheriff's office, Jeremiah said to Lester, 'We might just as well spend some of that cash those two had in their pockets. Let's take care of our animals first, and then maybe we can get a restaurant-cooked meal.'

Lester pointed down the street and said, 'Mr Jacobs' livery is not far.' He then pointed to the café across the street, 'Louise at the City Cafe puts out a good spread and the price is reasonable too.'

Jeremiah nodded in agreement, 'Afterwards we can get a room for the night. I could use a bath.'

Lester touched his arm. 'No need to go to the expense of a hotel room, Jeremiah. There is a good tub out at my place. It isn't far from here and it won't take long to heat up some water.'

Jeremiah nodded, 'All right, but won't we need to buy some supplies to take with us?'

Lester grinned, 'Yeah, the cupboards at home are bare, but Ben Atwood and Lenny Childers' pocket cash done provided us with the money to fill them up.'

At the City Café, when a young dark-haired waitress came to their table, Lester acknowledged her. 'Hello, Lucy. Bet you thought I was gone for good.'

'I knew that you had left town with your friend, that older man from Kansas City, Lester, but now you are back,' she said in wonder.

Lester nodded, 'Yes, I am back to stay this time, Lucy.'

'Well that is good news, Lester. How did all this happen in so short a time?'

'A lot has happened since I left with Mr Ticker, Lucy,' he explained. 'We were going to visit with my grand-mother in Kansas City when we stopped to rest about forty miles from here. I walked down to a lake for a swim. I just got into the water when I saw two men had just arrived where our horses were. I saw them shoot Mr Ticker in the back. They killed him and most likely would have killed me, but they could not find where I was hiding in the water. After a while, they left and took everything Ticker and I owned, horses and all, which left me afoot. A little later, Jeremiah,' he held a hand toward Jeremiah, 'came by and we got together. After we buried my friend, those same two killers caught us out on the road. They stopped us and said they were going take Jeremiah's carriage. I know they would have shot us dead, but Jeremiah and I took care of them instead. They are over at the undertak-ers right now.'

Jeremiah sat passively looking at the young woman while Lester explained.

Lucy blinked her eyes at Lester's declaration. 'I saw when you two rode in with those bodies on the horses. Did you kill them?' she asked.

Lester bobbed his head up and down, 'Me and Jeremiah did,' he declared.

She then turned to Jeremiah, 'Are you a gunman, sir?'

Jeremiah, a little bewildered by the young woman's question, shook his head, 'Far from it, ma'am. I just hap-pened along and was able to give Lester a hand taking care

98

of his friend's burying. Afterwards, those robbers stopped us on the road as Lester has said. I took exception to the robbers' threats and there was some shooting involved. We came out on top and the robbers didn't.'

'Well, I guess that is good. At least Lester looks no worse for wear.' She paused for a moment then turned to face Jeremiah. 'I'm Lucy Meadows. My mother Louise owns the café.'

Jeremiah bobbed his head, 'Pleased to meet you, Lucy. I'm Jeremiah Hackett,' he acknowledged.

Lucy smiled then extended her hand. Jeremiah stood and took her hand in his and shook it gently while staring into her eyes. He had become almost speechless by her charm and beauty. Lucy was five feet three, with dark hair, blue eyes and a smooth blemish-free face.

Jeremiah would not say that she was gorgeous, but she sure was darned pretty. Jeremiah had never spent any time around what he would term a decent town woman. He was never in one place that long to establish a relationship. One of the habits he had adopted from George Finimin was to spend some time with soiled doves whenever his male urges got the best of him. However, he could plainly see that Lucy Meadows was a lady and he did not want to talk to her in an indecent manner, so he had kept his answers short. Lucy had gotten his attention, that was for sure. She removed her hand from Jeremiah's then asked, 'What can I get for you two?'

'I told Jeremiah that we couldn't beat the daily special, Lucy and we do have money to pay.'

Lucy smiled, 'Why, Lester, you know that we'd never send you away hungry.'

They both ordered the daily special, which consisted of meat loaf, mashed potatoes with gravy and a vegetable. Buttermilk biscuits, coffee and a generous slice of apple pie topped out the meal.

While working on his slice of pie, Jeremiah asked Lester, 'Do you have any idea how much taxes are due on your place?'

Lester nodded, 'Me and Mr Ticker asked John Andrews before we left. He said it was around a hundred dollars. I wanted to stick around and get some kind of work so's I could pay the tax bill off, but nobody in town had enough need to hire me for more than my daily food bill. About that time, Ticker came to town and that was when I agreed to go back to Grandmother's place with him. It was my aim to ask Grandmother to loan me the money until I could pay her back.'

Jeremiah nodded, 'I can front the money until we get the rewards, if you want.'

Lester shook his head. 'I was told that we got until the end of the month before Andrews would pay it off and take the place as bank property.'

At the Cummings' farm the house, barn and small corral appeared well built and rather well cared for, with no loose siding boards or broken windows, and the front door closed tight. The barn had a bit of a saggy roof and couple of corral posts looked to be leaning, but then every place always needed a little upkeep, Jeremiah surmised. From the appearance of things, it did indeed indicate that Lester had left his home with the intent to return.

Lester pointed for Jeremiah to pull the carriage up near the front door for ease of unloading the supplies that they had just bought. In a short time, the goods were unloaded. Jeremiah saw to the care of Chelsea and Lester's two horses while Lester busied inside the house. Lester put away the supplies, then kindled a fire to heat some water for Jeremiah's bath.

The next morning, Lester gave Jeremiah a tour of the farm; it was just that, a farm in need of someone to work the fields, but it appeared to be a good place to live. Jeremiah liked the place and was happy enough that things worked out that he could stay there with Lester. In his estimation, the place could become profitable by growing and marketing the right kind of crops.

Two days later, Jeremiah and Lester, hopeful to conclude their business with the sheriff, entered the lawman's office.

After initial greetings, McDaniel held a hand out to two chairs facing his desk. Jeremiah and Lester sat. McDaniel wasted no time in preliminaries by pushing a receipt book across the desk then pointed to the open book. 'All you have to do is sign the book for my records then you can go over to the bank and collect the rewards. I can go with you, if you want.'

He cast a glance to Lester to let him know that if the split did not happen as agreed then he would ensure that it did.

Jeremiah quickly read the receipt, made out in his name alone, and then he picked up the proffered ink pen and signed his name while Lester watched.

'No need for you to come with us, Sheriff; Lester and I can handle things. We'll set up an account in his name and get his taxes paid.'

McDaniel nodded, 'Very well. Now, I did receive a wire from Lester's grandmother. According to her, Lester's stepmother no longer lives with her and has since moved on. Mrs Olsen indicated the loss of her long-time friend and employee Melvin Ticker upset her. I worded the missive to her in a fashion that indicated that Lester had come into money enough to sustain himself and that you

101

had agreed to his guardianship and would be staying with him on the farm. She understood Lester's want to stay at the farm and make a go of things and said it was OK by her. All she asked was that Lester write her a letter. I believe she'd like to know the details on how Ticker died and would like to know something more about his new guardian.'

Jeremiah and Lester both nodded.

'That's fine, Sheriff,' Jeremiah said.

'I'll send her a letter in the next day or so,' Lester promised.

John Andrews at the bank was surprised, but happy to pay out the reward money. He turned to Jeremiah and asked, 'How would you like to be paid, Mr Hackett? I would suggest a bank draft, which is good at any bank. . . .'

'Actually, sir,' Jeremiah cut him off, 'I am going to be around for an unknown time. By authority of Sheriff McDaniel, I am now Lester's guardian but prefer to think of he and I as partners. I prefer that the money remain in your bank with the distribution as follows: $900 placed in an account under Lester's name only, and then he can settle what taxes are due on his property. Put another $900 in an account under my name only. I'd like the remaining $200 in cash.'

John Andrews's eyebrows went up while listening to this informative revelation, but did not question Jeremiah's directive. He was very happy to have new money into his bank.

Jeremiah looked on as Andrews set up the accounts, then reduced Lester's account by $87 for the taxes due on the property. As soon as Jeremiah received the $200 in cash, he counted out $100 and handed it to Lester.

'Pocket money,' he proclaimed.

Once out on the street, Jeremiah and Lester began walking the boardwalks. Jeremiah remembered when George Finimin had bought him a new set of clothes. He pointed a finger across the street toward Allendale's Mercantile. 'Why don't we go over there and get you a new change of clothes and a hat, Lester. I'll pay.'

Before Lester could object, he explained, 'Since I am living with you now, Lester, I have to pay my way somehow.'

'You already paid for all those supplies we took home, that would be enough. I do need some new duds, but I'll pay for my own clothes.'

Jeremiah did not argue.

CHAPTER 15

The two spent the following month at the farm. During the day, Jeremiah and Lester worked side by side to shore up the saggy barn roof, care for their respective animals and other chores. One chore was cutting and gathering firewood, which took considerable time. They used the horse that had belonged to Lester's father to pull the sled built for hauling cut wood to the house. At night, Jeremiah inventoried the saleable goods he had in the carriage. He was short on some items but the way things had worked out, he did not see the need to make a long trip to St Louis to stock up. He knew he could wire the jobber with an order to have the merchandise delivered to Hays City; that, of course, would happen only after he sent the appropriate money to cover the costs. Jeremiah saw no need to do that right away, after all, he had not made any recent sales. Fact was, as he thought back, the last sale he had made was to a man and woman traveling through town back in Ellsworth. He was not worried about making a profit by selling some goods as in the past. With the reward money that he had collected on Basham and Ryan, along with the split reward he and Lester had collected on Childers and Atwood, he could go a long time before feeling a pinch.

It was now the beginning of winter and though Jeremiah, used to a lot of travel, was a bit itchy to hit the road, he figured that staying in a comfortable farmhouse during the cold of winter was not so bad. After all, he had spent last winter at Blanchards' place and things had worked out better than he could have hoped. At some point, though, he would have to head out on the road in order to get the business rolling again and resume his quest to find Emil Croft. He did not want to endanger Lester, but if he were to hit the road, because he had agreed to guardianship, Lester would have to accompany him. With that thought in mind, Jeremiah figured to spend the down time of winter indoctrinating and showing Lester how to prepare and bottle the various mixtures. Jeremiah did not have enough bottles to fill, but was able to secure a few empty bottles from the pharmacy in town. Jeremiah provided Lester with a list of the items that he was offering for sale with the price beside each item. He also had a stack of papers, provided by the jobber in St Louis, which gave instructions of dosages for potential customers. The instructions would help to eliminate the need to hawk each item's curative qualities to the curious, which Jeremiah never did like doing, though George Finimin loved to verbalize. Lester proved to be a good student and helper, eager in fact, just as Jeremiah had been under the tutelage of George Finimin.

The two fell into a routine of working all week, then venturing into town for a meal at the City Café on Saturday. If Jeremiah were in town on his own, he would have had three meals a day at the café, if only to see and talk with Lucy Meadows. He figured that it was a good thing that he was staying out at Lester's place. One such Saturday afternoon in February, Jeremiah offered to accompany Lester into town and sponsor their weekly meal at the favored eatery.

Lester grinned when giving his acceptance, 'I'm more than ready for some of Louise's cooking and I'll bet Lucy will be happy to see you as well.' He grinned even wider, knowing the attraction of Lucy and Jeremiah to each other and of their Saturday night meetings after the restaurant closed. He secretly hoped the two would become involved. That would be one good way to anchor Jeremiah to Hays City. Jeremiah would meet Lucy after the restaurant closed. The two would walk around town a bit, then he would walk her home. At times, in mid-week, Jeremiah would take the carriage to town and pick Lucy up, then the two would ride around the countryside, stopping by a gurgling stream for a picnic. Jeremiah, at first, was reluctant to discuss his past with Lucy and she had not pressed him to do so. As the two became more familiar with each other, however, Lucy began to ask questions, such as where he came from, where was his family, and how had he become a potion salesman. Eventually, Jeremiah told her of his upbringing, then leaving his uncle's farm and meeting up with George Finimin, but did not go into Finimin's murder.

Then one day she said, 'Jeremiah, I know that you and Lester had no choice but to shoot those men you brought to town, but from what I have seen, you are not a killer by nature. You seem to be a nice enough man, but I do not believe that you came all the way to Hays City just to sell potions.'

Jeremiah thought for a moment to evade the question, then relented and told her everything, beginning with Finimin's murder.

'So, continuing to sell potions has become just a smoke screen while you search for Emil Croft,' Lucy said. 'And

along the way, you eliminated some very bad men and collected money for doing so.'

Jeremiah nodded, 'I did not plan on that happening
and it's just the way things have worked out.'

With the prospect of going to town, Jeremiah and Lester
spent a little time cleaning themselves and changing from
their rough work clothes into more presentable attire. In
his usual waistcoat, with pin-striped pants tucked inside his
calf-high boots, Jeremiah looked at his boots then raised
each foot to swipe the face of the boot across the back of
his opposite leg. It was not polish but at least the dust was
gone.

Lester changed into his newly purchased chambray
shirt, canvas pants and a suit jacket similar to Jeremiah's
outfit.

Before saddling the father's horse, Jeremiah scooped a
generous portion of grain into a manger for Chelsea to
munch on while they were gone.

They rode into town at a leisurely pace, then nosed the
horses in front of Louise's City Café. They had no more
than tied their reins to the hitch pole when Sheriff
McDaniel appeared on the boardwalk fronting the café.

'Good, I caught you in time,' he said.

Jeremiah looked at him questioningly. The sheriff
stood still, 'There's a young wannabe gunslinger in town,
with a partner, and they've been asking about you. I've
already had a word with them, but thought I'd warn you,
just in case.'

Jeremiah nodded, 'Well, if they've been here for a few
days, they already learned where I'm staying. Lester and I
haven't had any visitors, Sheriff, so maybe they are just
curious.'

Daniel shook his head, 'Oh they know where you live,

enough folks have already told them, but their kind wouldn't try anything like back-shooting or such. They want an audience and that means calling you out in public for all to see.'

Jeremiah pulled both sides of his waistcoat aside, 'I haven't worn my gun to town since you advised me against doing that.'

He did, however, have the .41 caliber derringer he had taken from Lenny Childers' boot in his right-hand pocket and out of sight.

McDaniel nodded, 'Well, I'm glad that you listened. This is serious business, Jeremiah. That one calls himself Slick Wells. I did a little checking. Not so long ago, down in Garden City, he goaded a drink-filled farmer into drawing an old Walker Colt cap-and-ball six-gun against him. It was not any kind of contest. Hell, a Walker Colt weighs four and half pounds and has a nine-inch barrel. The old hand cannon would be cumbersome to say the least. The farmer did not even clear leather before he was bleeding out and lay dying in the street. The ones that witnessed the killing said it was plain suicide or murder, whatever way you look at it. Now Slick is looking to extend his reputation for all to see. I'd be willing to bet that he will seek you out as soon as he learns that you are in town.'

'OK, Sheriff, Lester and I just came to town to get a meal that we didn't cook for ourselves, but I will be on the watch. Rest assured though, I have no intention of borrowing a six-gun and drawing against him to prove his point.'

Jeremiah and Lester had just finished their meal of steak, potatoes, gravy and bread, and were set to dig into their apple pie dessert when two young men, dressed as ordinary cowboys walked through the door. Jeremiah noticed that both men were armed. The one known as Slick, wearing all black, led the way, while his partner, dressed in a blue chambray shirt and jeans, followed two steps behind. Slick stepped to stand in front of Jeremiah's table. Slick was tall, maybe five foot ten, and skinny. He had long dirty-blond hair pulled back in a ponytail behind his head. He had a sun-scarred sharp-featured face and yellowish coyote-like eyes. The young man behind him was shorter and heavier. He had sweat running down the blotchy skin of his face. He held a worried look that spoke of fear.

Slick came to stand with his legs apart to shoulder width; some say it would be a gunman's stance. He worn a pair of six-guns, with the nose of the holsters tied low on each leg. Curiously, he chose to wear his six-guns with the handles facing forward for a cross-draw by either hand.

Jeremiah was not impressed, figuring the gunman had positioned his six-guns that way just as a matter of show to anyone watching. Jeremiah was no expert on gunfights, but it seemed to him that positioning one's six-gun so that he had to reach across his waist was not very smart. A gunman would do everything he could to shave time off his draw and a cross-draw was not the way to do it.

It was true that when Jeremiah wore his six-gun, it was in a cross-draw position across his stomach. He had purposefully positioned the weapon there for ease of drawing while seated, which proved beneficial when he had that deadly encounter with Ben Atwood. Jeremiah had never intended to draw his six-gun against someone for show, just to prove a point. However, here stood a man who figured to force the issue.

Slick stared at Jeremiah then spoke, 'Well, if it ain't Jeremiah Hackett, the famous gunman that took out Ben Atwood and Lenny Childers. My partner Stan and I just came over so that we could become acquainted with a man as famous as you.'

He paused for a moment while casting a glance around the room, possibly to see if anyone were watching. 'My name is Slick Wells. You no doubt have heard of me. Just hearing my name puts a scare in some folks because they know that I am a badass gunman who is fast on the draw. My name put a scare in you, Hackett?'

Jeremiah glared at the self-proclaimed gunman, 'No, I guess it don't. Fact is, before tonight, I never heard the name before.'

Slick attempted a smile but actually was seething with anger. His ego was hurt when Jeremiah did not acknowledge his name or his notoriety, which he had hoped was now common street talk.

Slick would have loved to shoot the blank-faced Jeremiah, who seemed unconcerned and now coolly turned his attention to eating his apple pie as if he had dismissed the man standing before him. Stan, who was watching when Jeremiah and Lester came to town, had already told Slick that Jeremiah had pulled his jacket tails up to show the sheriff that he was not wearing a six-gun.

Slick was aware that any gunfight would have to be by mutual consent of the two parties concerned. If he just up and shot Jeremiah, then that sheriff would arrest him. The sheriff had already told him and Stan that any show of gunplay would result in arrest and fines.

He figured to goad Jeremiah further, get him to strap on a six-gun and face off with him for all to see. However, Jeremiah did not seem to be ruffled at all and Slick lacked the knowledge of how to get him to change his mind.

Slick was not ready to give up yet. 'I suppose you came to town to spend some of the two thousand dollars you got for the bounty on those two. Maybe you ought to spread some of that wealth around; come over to the saloon and buy some drinks.'

Jeremiah chewed, then swallowed some pie, then picked up his coffee cup for a sip. 'I don't want a drink right now; got nothing to celebrate. I work hard for my money, the left-overs are invested over at the bank, where I can draw some interest,' he said, then went back to forking another bite of pie.

Stan reached a hand to touch Slick's shoulder, possibly in an effort to get him to let things go before he made himself look more foolish. Slick was quick to swat Stan's hand away.

'I'll see you again, Hackett. Count on it,' he said, then abruptly turned and stormed out the door with Stan following at his heels.'

Jeremiah and Lester had finished their meal when Lucy came to the table with a worried look on her face. 'I heard what that man said. He was trying to goad you into facing him. Is everything OK, Jeremiah?'

Jeremiah nodded, 'Everything is fine, Lucy. Lester and I were just leaving. We will go on back to the farm. That way there will not be a reason for that fella or others like him to make a nuisance of themselves.'

A week later when they came to town again for their Saturday meal, Sheriff McDaniel greeted them in front of the City Café. After exchanging greetings, Sheriff McDaniel said, 'No need to spend any time wondering about seeing that fella Slick again.'

Jeremiah raised his eyebrows. 'That so, Sheriff? What happened?'

Sheriff McDaniel grinned, 'Well this past Thursday night Slick had a few too many drinks and was bragging about his self. One of our citizens tired of hearing Slick mouthing off and said so. One thing led to another then Slick took a swing at the one man that he should have avoided.

'Those who watched said the fight did not last long. Reggie Crown the blacksmith ducked the punch that Slick had directed toward him, then put a meaty fist onto his nose. Reggie would have stopped at that but Slick, who was then lying on the floor, attempted to pull a six-gun. That move sure as hell infuriated Reggie. He stepped forward then proceeded to clean Slick's clock for him. Reggie broke Slick's right arm as if it was matchwood then dragged him over to the end of the bar and forced his face into a spittoon full of tobacco spit. When the deputies showed up, to quiet things down, Reggie was helping Slick's partner Stan to load Slick onto Stan's shoulder for a trip to the doc. Mid-morning the next day, Slick waited on his horse with his arm in a sling while Stan went into the saloon and fished both of Slick's six-guns out of spittoons. One of which was the same messy spittoon that Slick's face had been forced into last night. I did not see it, but deputy Krebbs said that the two of them rode out of town headed south. I do not expect to see them back. If he has not learned his lesson, then most likely Slick will heal up and try again. If he does, then he'll be a candidate for an early grave.'

CHAPTER 16

On an early April Monday morning, Jeremiah, with Lester sitting beside him, drove the carriage into Hays City and pulled up in front of the sheriff's office. The two climbed from their seat. Jeremiah secured Chelsea to a dropped weight while Lester checked on his horse tied by a lead rope to the back of the carriage.

Sheriff McDaniel, seated behind his desk, looked up when the door to the office opened. Lester, followed by Jeremiah entered.

'Morning, Sheriff,' Jeremiah offered while Lester mumbled the same.

The sheriff wondered what was the purpose of the visit, nodded, then said, 'Morning yourselves.'

'Just thought we'd check in with you before we take off,' Jeremiah began. 'Lester and I have been holed-up at the farm all winter and are now ready to do a little traveling. We plan to head up north on a sales trip and hopefully gain some information on Croft.'

McDaniel raised his eyebrows, 'How long you figure to be gone?'

Jeremiah shrugged a shoulder, 'Depends, I guess, on what we find, but I figure a month or two.'

Lester then stepped forward, 'George Watson is going

to stay out at my place and look out for things and take care of the animals.'

The sheriff straightened in his chair. 'George Watson is a drunk. You trust that he won't get careless with his drinking and smoking habit and burn the place down?'

Jeremiah flared a hand. 'George has been staying with us for couple of weeks now. He told us all about himself. I believe that he is happy as heck to have a place to call home and will take extra care of things.'

'Good, good,' McDaniel said. 'Maybe a new start is all the old man needs.' He flared a hand, 'Have a seat for a minute.'

McDaniel glanced out the window, 'I see that you are taking your carriage. That is good; it means you will be sticking to the roads. I guess there is no sense in me trying to talk you two out of going on a hunt for Croft. I can see that you are set to go. It would be advisable to maybe pal up with some freighters and travel in company with them as much as you can. Best be on the lookout though. Since you and Lester brought Childers and Atwood in, the thieving and killing of travelers have slowed to a trickle, but there are still some bad people working in the outlying areas. We may never be rid of them altogether.'

Jeremiah nodded, 'That's good advice, Sheriff.'

Jeremiah knew, however, that the majority of the freight haulers would be traveling the main roads that ran east and west rather than north.

McDaniel continued, 'Now, since you said you would be heading north of here, there is a place that you ought to know. About forty miles north-east of here is a trading post owned by a man named Ogden McGinty. He calls the place Broken Wagon. It is located out in the middle of nowhere at a crossroads east of Stockton by a dozen miles, just south of the South Fork of the Solomon River, but it is located on a good road to Colorado.

'We, the law anyway, believe that McGinty is a friend to outlaws, at least as long as the outlaw can place something in McGinty's palm. We suspect that he operates the place as a clearinghouse for stolen goods and gives sanctuary to those on the run. I believe that Atwood and Childers headed straight to McGinty's after pulling their robberies. This office and others working with the US Marshals service have attempted raids on the place after getting word of murders and thefts occurring in or near that area, but we were always too late. McGinty is shrewd; most likely has others watching all the roads to alert him to anyone traveling. Every time a force of officers has shown up, they find nothing incriminating. McGinty explains away tracks leading right to his place by saying, "There are lots of travelers on the road. I don't ask questions of no one, just sell them what they want and they ride away".

'He's keeps an inventory on hand of about anything a traveler would want, food, clothes, whiskey, a cheap woman for those inclined. He also keeps plenty of hand tools and such, some tack and a few firearms, but no traceable livestock or large stuff like wagons or furniture. By the time we get out there, any reported stolen wagons, plus the freight on board, any livestock, horses or mules are long gone. I figure he makes some kind of deal with the actual thieves, then has the stolen goods driven away immediately. Who his partner on the other end is and where he is located is a mystery we would love to solve. I have a hunch that the stuff ends up in Colorado; Denver most likely, or some other large town, which could provide plenty of opportunity for disposal.'

Jeremiah nodded, 'Well, if we learn anything Sheriff, we'll let you know.'

McDaniel pursed his lips, 'Another thing to note is that

115

a sneak thief by the name of Otis Rhodes might be in the area. Rhodes was serving a sentence for embezzlement and theft. He escaped prison along with Atwood and Childers. We are aware that Rhodes has previously done some disposal of stolen wagons, horses, jewelry and such. So, I'm inclined to believe that though he did not ride with Atwood and Childers on their raids, he is the link between the thieves and McGinty and the receivers of the stolen goods.'

Jeremiah's interest was now piqued, and he asked, 'Is there a wanted poster on Rhodes?'

The sheriff shuffled through a stack of posters from the corner of his desk. He extracted one and handed it across the desk to Jeremiah.

'Five hundred dollars offered for his capture.' He sat back then added, 'Notice it says for his capture and not dead or alive. Wouldn't want you to start shooting first and worry about the ramifications later. The man is a thief, not a killer.'

Figuring the meeting was over, Jeremiah, followed by Lester, stood and extended his hand. 'Thanks, Sheriff. We'll be seeing you.'

The two then went to Louise's restaurant. Jeremiah wanted to say goodbye to Lucy. He had already told Lucy of his intent to leave for a while this past Saturday night. Lester intended to get Lucy or Louise to provide a meal for his and Jeremiah's supper on the road.

Lucy hugged Jeremiah then stood back, 'You come back to me, Jeremiah.'

He promised to do so.

When seated on the carriage, the two headed out of town by a route that took them straight north from Hays City toward Stockton, some forty miles distance. Jeremiah figured about half that distance would be enough travel-ing for the day before making a camp for the night.

It was mid-afternoon when Jeremiah noticed that Chelsea had worked up a sweat and was beginning to lather under the leather riggings. He scanned ahead in search of any greenery that would indicate a source of water. He guided Chelsea off to the left to a draw where some bushes had grown eight feet high along a creek bed that had very little water in it, maybe an inch or so – not much, but it would do. Jeremiah busied himself unhook-ing Chelsea and rubbing her down with a gunnysack. When done, he knew she would not wander far, so he turned her loose to check out the water on her own. Lester was busy gathering wood, mostly small sticks scat-tered nearby, to make a campfire. There wasn't enough wood available to keep a fire going all night but the spring weather was warm enough that they didn't feel the need anyway.

The small fire was enough to make coffee and heat up the meal that Lester had Louise prepare for them while Jeremiah was saying good-bye to Lucy. After they had their supper, the two sat supping coffee.

'You figure we'll make Stockton tomorrow?' Lester asked.

Jeremiah nodded, 'Yeah, I figured we would get a room and a meal there, maybe stay another night or so. I would like to spend a little time asking the locals about Croft. I can set up the carriage for sales, if you want to try selling something while I am asking around.'

Lester grinned, 'Sure, I'd like that.'

CHAPTER 17

Stockton, Kansas, was a newly developed town, established in 1872 by some enterprising merchants. The town had grown measurably and had incorporated as a city this past year of 1879. City officials were hopeful of attracting the railroad to make Stockton a stopping point in their east-west route.

Jeremiah and Lester stood before the counter at the Metropole Hotel. The clerk said they would find accommodations for their animals at the Three Cs stable directly behind the hotel. He also gave directions to the local marshal's office. Jeremiah paid for the room with two beds then turned to Lester and handed him the key.

'Lester, why don't you take the carriage and see to Chelsea's care at that stable while I check in with the local law? I'll meet you at the stable in a little while,' Jeremiah said.

Lester bobbed his head in acknowledgement then they both walked out the door.

Jeremiah entered the marshal's office on the east end of town. Emmett Grosser, the marshal, was a thirty-five-year-old rangy-looking man whose appearance bespoke of a former life of ranch work, perhaps a cowboy. Grosser was a friendly man, giving a hardy shake to Jeremiah's hand.

'Always glad to see new faces in town,' he proclaimed.

Jeremiah introduced himself then told of his tonic business. 'I and my associate will be around town a few days. Would there be any problem with me parking my carriage on one of the streets and make a few sales?'

Grosser thought for a moment then shook his head side to side, 'I see no problem, Jeremiah, as long as no one complains about the tonics afterwards. There is an empty lot down the street across from the barbershop. You could park your rig there, if you want.'

Out of curiosity and courtesy Jeremiah asked, 'Have you been here long, Marshal?'

Grosser shook his head, 'Actually, I'm a new hire on. I come from Texas. I came here after delivering a herd to Ogallala. I was on my way back to Texas; spent the night here and heard they were looking to hire a marshal. Well, the next day I applied for the job and they hired me. I've been on the job nigh on to a month now.'

Jeremiah did not feel like giving his other reason for being in this county and have to explain all over again all about his vendetta to find Emil Croft, then suffer through a reprimand again for doing so. He figured it would be better to find someone who had been here for long period to get the information he needed. He stood then asked, 'Is there someone in town who has been here for a time that might know more about the county that I can talk to? I don't want to spend my time driving off in search of a farm or ranch and find out I went in the wrong direction and end up on barren land or, worse yet, get lost.'

Grosser thought for a moment, 'You ought to talk to Jig Riley down at the livery. I believe that he has been here the longest. He knows everyone around here and he will talk your ear off telling you so. He might even let you park your rig in front of his place. That would be a good spot to make some sales. Lots of folks go by there.'

119

Jeremiah nodded, he already knew that bartenders and livery owners always seemed to know everything that went on around the surrounding country.

Jeremiah smiled then stuck out his hand again, 'Thanks for the tip, Marshal. It looks like you found a good home. I'll try not to be a bother.'

Grosser shook Jeremiah's hand in acknowledgement, 'I'm glad you stopped by. Most of those who come to town usually try to avoid talking to me. Good luck to you.'

Jeremiah observed the buildings and streets as he walked back toward the hotel and livery. It was certainly a prosperous-looking town and well maintained. The streets were free of weeds and horse droppings. Two of the buildings looked freshly built and all appeared in good shape. Some had whitewashed fronts and all the boardwalks were level and swept clean.

When he walked through the wide doors of the Three Cs livery, Jeremiah saw the carriage parked inside the building and that Lester was brushing Chelsea's sides while the animal stood munching oats from a manger. He was also carrying on a conversation, or rather listening, to a well-apportioned man of perhaps fifty years dressed in a chambray shirt and denim pants. He wore a well-worn flat brimmed hat with curled edges. Seated on a hay bale behind Lester, the man was gabbing away.

'I haven't seen one them little hinnies in a long time. That is a fine looking little animal. There ain't another one in the county that I know about.' The older man said without pause. 'Most folks I know of go for the biggest mule they can get and expect the animal to take on giant loads. Course ye wouldn't want to put much of load on that little muley. Why, I seen the time. . . .'

'I take it that you've been in this country for a fairly long time?' Jeremiah cut in to stop the talkative man from going into a lengthy tall tale.

The man bobbed his head. 'Name's Jig Riley. I've been here twenty-five years or so. I set this shop up to take care of all those wandering pilgrims heading out to Oregon and California. I was one of them travelers myself. Back then, I was a young man full of vigor and looking for adventure and a better life. I helped one of my fellow travelers fix his wagon wheel that had busted and then another fellow stepped up and said that he needed some help too. Said he would pay me to work on his rig that had a loose wheel. Before I finished, another fellow showed up with a problem, so I made up my mind to settle right here. Figured I could do just as well here as going on out to Oregon. I built this here barn and the town kinda grew up around me. Yes sir. . . .'

Before the man could get himself wound up again, Jeremiah stepped forward and stuck out his hand, 'Jeremiah Hackett. Lester and I are traveling together. We'll be around for a day or so and hopefully sell some of our wares.'

Jig Riley gave him a firm handshake. 'I already met Lester. He looks to be a fine young man. I have seen all kinds of peddlers coming through town hawking everything from plows to whiskey to windmills, but you are the first tonic salesman that has come through. Where did you boys come from?'

'Oh, I'm from back east,' Jeremiah, said. 'St Louis is sort of home base, but I have been down to Lester's place near Hays City of late. Say, would you happen to know anything about a fella named Emil Croft? I was told he had a place somewhere in this neck of the woods.'

Jig Riley frowned. 'I hope you are not kin to him,' he said sourly.

'No, I am not related, by any means,' Jeremiah assured

121

sternly. 'I am looking to locate him and settle a private matter.'

Jig Riley's facial features relaxed somewhat, but his demeanor was stern. 'Well, I do know of him. Fact is, I'd like to run across him. He owed me money for taking care of his mules for a week, then skipped out without paying. If him and those two no-account whelps that ride with him ever show....'

Jeremiah's heart skipped a beat. This was the first lead he had ever gotten on Croft.

'Does Croft have a homestead or farm located around here?' Jeremiah cut in again.

Jig Riley nodded, 'I know that he had a place a few miles out of town west of here, located on the other side of that trading post that Ogden McGinty set up, but I don't know if Emil still owns it or not. I know he left the country for a time.'

Jeremiah nodded, 'Yes, he did. I am looking to locate him for something he did down in Arkansas nearly two years ago.'

Jig Riley's eyes flared, 'Well, whatever Emil Croft did, I don't figure was anything good. McGinty is out there all the time; he might know more than I do, that is if you can get him to talk. Most likely, he will not say anything about a customer unless Croft stiffed him too. McGinty calls that place of his Broken Wagon. He has been there for near about as long as I have been here in Stockton. McGinty set himself up on the road out there as a goods trader. After a time, he hired a man to do some minor wagon repairs for travelers to get them on their way, but I end up doing most of the blacksmithing, the jobs that call for a forge. Folks know that I have a good forge and a full-time helper for the big jobs to boot. I figure that McGinty was trying to offer all the services he could and maybe take all my business away. I never worried too much about that. Folks soon learned that he did not give a damn about caring for animals and blacksmithing work like I do. As far as I know McGinty spends all his time trading what goods he's got or selling whiskey and a loose woman to travelers.'

Jeremiah nodded, 'I have heard about McGinty's place, but the one that I am after is Emil Croft. He owes a debt that I intend to collect.'

Jig Riley glared at Jeremiah, 'Does he owe you money too?'

Jeremiah shook his head, 'He killed my former partner, for no good reason, sometime back. Until recent, I couldn't come after him, but now I feel it is the time to catch up to him.'

Before Jig Riley could reply, a man seated with a woman beside him on a buckboard pulled up out front. Riley began to step away toward the buckboard.

Jeremiah wanted to talk with the man some more, but it would have to wait. 'I can see that you are busy, but I'd like to buy you a supper, maybe a beer later, if you care to,' he offered.

Jig Riley stopped and turned to face Jeremiah. 'I'd like that. I will be through here about seven. I can meet you over to Fourth Street Café. I take all my meals there and the food is good and plenty.'

Jeremiah nodded, 'Lester and I will be there.'

Jeremiah and Lester put Chelsea and Lester's horse in the open corral next to the livery then went to their hotel room. Each spent some time cleaning while waiting for their supper appointment.

Jeremiah and Lester left the hotel at six-thirty and walked the block and a half to the Fourth Street Café. When a middle-aged matronly woman, with her grey-streaked hair in a bun greeted them, Jeremiah said, 'We are here to have supper with Jig Riley when he's finished over at the livery.'

The woman smiled, 'Good, maybe he can talk your ear off instead of mine. We love having Jig here, but he sure likes to talk on and on when I still got work to do for the night. Can I bring you some coffee or something until he shows up? I do not imagine that it will be long. We got ham, sweet potatoes, green beans and biscuits, and peach cobbler for dessert tonight.'

'That sounds great. Coffee for me,' Jeremiah said. Lester nodded for the same.

Jig Riley came in when Jeremiah and Lester were on their second cup of coffee. He called out over his shoulder as he strode toward the table, 'Go ahead and start bringing the food out, Velma. I'm as hungry as a bear.'

He plopped into a chair facing Jeremiah. Lester sat between the two men.

'Howdy again, gents,' Riley offered.

'Glad you could make it, Jig,' Jeremiah said. Lester mumbled a greeting.

Velma apparently knew Jig's habits, immediately placing a plate of the night's fare before him, together with a cup of coffee. Behind her, a short bald man wearing an apron, presumably the cook, stepped forward to place plates of food before Jeremiah and Lester.

The three ate their meal in silence.

Ten minutes later, Jig, his plate emptied, sat back and gave a sigh as he reached for his coffee cup. 'That was damn fine. They always do a good job here.'

Lester was still working on the cobbler. Jeremiah had finished his and used a napkin to blot against his mouth. 'Yes, it was a great meal.'

Jig Riley nodded, 'I haven't seen Emil Croft since he left here, must be all of two years ago now. Old Mort over at the Plains Relief saloon told me that Emil and another fella stopped in for a couple beers last fall, but he has not mentioned anything since. He knows that Emil stiffed me and I know he would tell me if he had seen him of late.'

'Thanks for telling me what you know,' Jeremiah said. 'It looks like my best bet is to go on over to Broken Wagon and nose around a bit. Croft may very well be living back at his old homestead, which you said wasn't far from the trading post.'

Jig Riley nodded his understanding. 'Better be careful. That is a rough damned place. Some two and half years back, I did a little deputy work for the then Marshal John Hames. Hames recruited me and two other deputies to participate in a sweep conducted by the US Marshal to clean up the lawlessness in the four counties that make up this area. Hames already knew that McGinty's trading post was a haven for all kinds of riff-raff. He was a likable young fella, like you and raring to go. I guess he wanted to make a good impression because he had me and two other posse men ride out to Broken Wagon without waiting for the Deputy US Marshals to show up and accompany us. Turns out that was a mistake. There were four horses tied up out front, so Hames identified himself and called for the owners to step outside. Come to find out it was a gang of four no-goods sitting there inside McGinty's trading post drinking whiskey. As soon as Hames called for them to come out, one of them answered by shooting a six-gun through a window. The bullet hit Hames in the chest and knocked him off his horse. The rest of us dived for cover. Then all hell broke loose. All four of those bastards were throwing lead at us. I took a bullet to my leg but I got four shots off, one of which killed one of the no-goods but I do not know if he was the one that shot Hames. My posse partners riddled another one with lead, but the other two made a break for it and got clean away. Things happened so fast, I never got a look at any of their faces, until we rolled over the two we had killed. By the time we had things sorted out and attempted to give Hames some care, dang if he didn't up and die from that .44 slug he took to one of his lungs. He was a good man. I was in a bad way. I had a hole in my leg and I was bleeding out fast. The other members of the posse put a tourniquet on my leg, then hauled me fast as they could back to Stockton to the doctor's office. Two Deputy US Marshals showed up the next day. They interviewed me and the others, then they rode out to McGinty's place. Of course, McGinty himself pled innocent of any wrongdoing and ignorance of knowledge of the other two that got away. He claimed that all he did was to sell some drinks to some travelers. The two escapers might have been Croft and that oldest boy of his, I would not put it past them. The last time I seen that boy he acted like I was his servant and he treated the mules they had in harness badly.'

He paused for a moment then continued, 'I don't have much use for a man that mistreats his animals. I figured that he is as mean as a snake. The other one, the younger one, was always quiet, seemed kinda slow in the thinker, if you asked me.'

'Neither of those boys will be a bother to anyone ever again.' Jeremiah stated flatly.

'How's that?' Jig Riley asked with a look of wonder in his eye.

Jeremiah paused for a moment to consider things before answering. He figured that Jig Riley looked as if he was a reasonable man and he was the only person that he had located who knew of Emil Croft. If he was to locate

Croft then he had to put his trust in someone.

Jeremiah decided to tell the man.

'For the simple reason that I killed them both,' he declared.

Jig's eyes open wide with surprise at Jeremiah's news. 'You said Emil Croft killed your partner. Did his boys help Emil to do it?'

Jeremiah nodded, 'That's the reason they died.'

He further considered that it would do no harm to tell the whole story about George Finimin's death. He told of the four men coming to his and George's darkened camp, then their involvement in killing George Finimin. He went on to tell how he had tried to exact retribution later that very night. He told how he had stalked the camp. Wanting and believing that he would shoot Emil where he lay, but instead shot and killed the oldest son Clarence. Jeremiah then told how he clubbed Judson to death and how the main culprit Emil Croft had escaped. Jeremiah finished telling his rendition of the events with a sigh.

'Like you said earlier, Jig, things happen fast. I did what I felt was the right thing to do at the time.'

Just retelling the events of that loathsome night brought Jeremiah to a renewed seething anger.

'And you've been looking for that skunk ever since!' Jig exclaimed.

Jeremiah took a deep breath to calm himself, then bobbed his head in agreement. 'I wanted to get right on Emil's trail right away, but I didn't know for sure if the Mennings would talk to the law about the incident, so I had no choice but to leave that country behind. I was flat broke at the time, so I just left and began to carry on what George had taught me to do, which is to sell tonic for my daily bread. I put the hunt for Croft off until I was better equipped and financially able to go after him. I think about what happened every day and I will not stop until I find him.'

'The law ought to have done something,' Jig noted.

'If I told them, I figure they would most likely arrest me for killing the two sons and Emil would continue to go on his murderous way,' Jeremiah replied.

Jig nodded.

'You got a point there. As you already figured, the law can get in the way of settling matters the right way.' He paused for a moment. 'Lester said you went to see our local marshal. I could have saved you the visit. Emmett Grosser is a good enough man for the job of marshalling the streets here in town. He takes the job seriously. He and Old Judge Wilson are thick as fleas. I know they have a meeting at least every week. The judge, knowing that Grosser is new at law enforcement, sees to it that the man runs things strictly by the book. Grosser can be a real asshole at times. On more than one occasion, he has let some complaining folks, who live outside town limits, know that any law-breaking outside the town is the county sheriff's responsibility. In that, he is right, but he did not need to say it. It just does not seem right. Emmett is new to this area. He doesn't know anything about things that have gone on around here for years.'

'I merely introduced myself to the marshal as a potion salesman,' Jeremiah replied. 'He told me he was new to the area, so I did not mention anything about my looking for Emil Croft. I figured that he would not understand.'

'No, he wouldn't,' Jig replied. 'He'd only be looking at it from the side of the law and you'd be hard-pressed to explain the situation.'

Jeremiah nodded, 'Guess I'll cross that bridge when I cross it.'

'What makes you think you can take Croft?' Jig Riley

128

asked, 'I mean most folks would take you for an honest, clean young man just trying to make a living selling your tonic.'

Jeremiah smiled, 'I guess you could say that I don't look the part of a man who would purposely go up against a known killer, but I figure that fact gives me an advantage.'

'How do you figure that?' Jig Riley asked.

Jeremiah took the time to tell the man about his encounter with Bill Ryan and Tucker Basham.

Jig Riley raised his eyebrows. 'That was gutsy what you did to those two, but what about facing down a known killer who is ready to shoot you? Are you any good with a six-gun?'

Jeremiah nodded, 'Like I said, I equipped myself, bought a six-gun and practised shooting until I could hit something. It took a while and a lot of bullets to accomplish that.'

He then went on to tell all about how he came upon Lester by that abandoned way station and later the demise of Lenny Childers and Ben Atwood.

When Jeremiah had finished, Jig Riley raised his eyebrows. 'Well, you sure got the guts to do about anything you want, I'd say.'

He sat back for a moment, seemingly in deep thought. After a moment of silence, he said, 'Gutsy or no, I don't think it would be a good idea for you to drive your carriage out to Broken Wagon. You would be endangering yourself as well as Lester. I think that if Croft spotted your rig, he would most likely recognize it from the incidents in Arkansas that you described. If he did recognize you and felt threatened, I believe that he might try to ambush you from cover or shoot you when your back is turned. He's a yellow dog if there ever was one.'

Jeremiah listened without comment.

Jig Riley took a breath then said, 'It would be best if you had one or two others to go with you and just ride in on horseback as if you were just travelers stopping by for a drink or two. That would give you time to look things over and to see what kind of rats are sitting around.'

Jeremiah nodded, 'That's probably good advice, Jig. I'll keep that in mind.'

The hint of a smile tugged at the corners of Jig Riley's mouth. 'But you'll do it your way, no matter what.'

Jeremiah nodded and grinned.

CHAPTER 18

Jeremiah spent the next day in town. He wanted to familiarize himself with the rest of the town and see if anyone else knew of anything that might help in his search for Emil Croft. In addition, he wanted to get Lester situated to see how he would handle selling the tonics they had brought along. After spending a full morning asking questions, he learned from a barber that Croft had been in town last fall, same as Jig Riley had stated. Others that he had asked were either new to the area or did not pay attention to affairs outside of the city.

It was about noontime so he figured to go fetch Lester so the two of them could get a meal. When Jeremiah turned to walk to the livery, he could see that Lester had already pulled the carriage outside and parked to the left of the entrance. He was handing two bottles of something down to an older woman while the man next to her was extending two dollar bills toward Lester.

Jeremiah stepped to one side at the livery's entrance. He did not want to interfere with Lester's dealing.

Jeremiah felt a presence beside him. Jig Riley stepped to stand next to him and said, 'That Lester is a regular go-getter. He got here right after breakfast, spent an hour feeding and brushing down the mule then helped feed the other stock that I have boarded here. He mentioned setting up the rig to do some selling. I helped roll the carriage out and he has been doing a lively business since. It's a good spot.'

'Thanks, Jig, that is kindly of you. I'd be happy to pay you something . . .'

'Don't even think of it,' Jig cut in.

About that time Lester, smiling broadly, stepped forward to join Jig and Jeremiah. Before Jeremiah could commend him for making some potion sales of his own, Jig began speaking to Jeremiah. 'About our conversation last night; I was wide awake most of the night thinking about things, things that should have been resolved a long time ago. It still bothers me that Marshal Hames was shot and killed out at the McGinty place and how two of the shooters got away like they did. Nobody did a follow-up to track them down so the whole episode just up and died as if it never happened. I guess everyone, including me, figured that the US Marshal would see to it, but it just did not happen.

'It appears to me that you are the only one with an interest in righting some things. Well, sir, I would like to get in on running them yahoos down, especially if I could collar Emil Croft for avoiding his obligations. What say I ride out there with you, Jeremiah? I have not been out to that trading post since that dust-up that got Hames killed. I wouldn't mind seeing how ole McGinty's is getting along. I already know some of the men that hang out there and you are not likely to find them in church come Sunday morning. If you and Lester, being strangers, go stepping inside that den of rats, you might find that trouble could come your way as soon as you let your guard down. Some of the miscreants that hang out there will remember me from when I did the deputy work and won't be apt to start anything that they know I would finish for them.'

He paused for a moment as if to see of any objections, but before Jeremiah could say anything, Jig continued, 'Let me assure you that I will not get in your way. It's just that I would like to be of help. I know that I'm getting older and I got a bum leg, but I can still handle a six-gun and I would watch your back.'

Jig flared a hand in Lester's direction while talking to Jeremiah. 'I know you told me how Lester stood with you to corral those two killers, but I would need someone to help my hired hand, Elmer, at the livery while we're gone. I saw how Lester took right to taking care of your mule when you came to town and he done told me he has worked at a livery before. Elmer does the blacksmith work, but someone has to take in the work and Lester would do fine, I figure. You and I could ride out on horses and leave your carriage right here. Lester could stay as busy as he wants to be and he would be safe from any wild shots, if that were to happen.'

With Jig Riley staring silently at him, Jeremiah bobbed his head. Fact of the matter he did not get much sleep himself last night. There were too many things on his mind. For one he was delighted that he had located someone that knew of Croft. Second, he was hesitant to take Lester along on what could be a dangerous undertaking. He'd had those thoughts back in Hays City but couldn't figure out a way to part from Lester and the obligation he had taken on to be his guardian. Now Jig had proposed a way that would ensure Lester's safety and give himself some protection as well. To him it was the perfect solution – if only Lester would go along with it.

'I like it, Jig,' Jeremiah said. He then turned to face Lester. 'My partner Lester needs to approve of this though.' He paused a moment then added, 'Would you mind if Jig and I was gone for the day, Lester?'

Lester frowned, 'I was hoping that I could help you catch Croft. There might be others like Lenny Childers that would shoot you.'

Jeremiah grimaced, 'Lester, you and I are partners for sure, but I owe it to you and the promise I made to Sheriff McDaniel as your guardian to keep you safe. We are both new here. Jig is the only one that is familiar with the county and has said that he would need someone to help run the business while he is gone. Besides, we are just going to look things over. I am asking you as your friend to watch over Chelsea and do what you can for Jig?'

Lester hesitated for a moment then spoke without apprehension, 'If that's what you want, Jeremiah, I have no problem with doing as you say. I ain't afraid to go along, but it sounds like Jig wants to go there himself. I'll do whatever needs doing here in town. I kinda like running between the carriage and the livery.'

Jeremiah nodded then turned to face Jig, 'When would be a good time for us to go, Jig?'

Jig put a hand to his chin, 'Well, let's see. It's about a two-hour ride out to McGinty's place. By the time we get a meal and get our horses saddled, we can be on the road in, say, an hour. We will ride out to Croft's place first; see who is living there and if they are now the owners. Afterwards, we will double back to the trading post. By late afternoon, we will be able to get a good look at anyone inside the place. McGinty will be the busiest then, what with everyone looking to get to drinking. Now, if we do that, I think we would be wise to take along a blanket and a coffee pot, in case we are delayed and end up sleeping in a ravine.'

Jeremiah bobbed his head, 'I'll stop by the hotel, and get my jacket, guns and a blanket.'

Jig nodded, 'Let's go eat. I'll get Velma to fix us a carry-along meal for our supper tonight. Just a minute, before we go eat, let me tell Elmer to saddle us a couple horses. That way, when we finished eating our noon meal, we will be all set to leave.'

Jeremiah shoved the double-barreled shotgun into the saddle boot on the horse that Jig indicated was for his use. If possible, Jeremiah would like to be responsible for Emil Croft's demise. If possible, in the same manner that Croft had done to George Finimin, which was swift and without compunction. Jeremiah also belted on his six-gun. Jig Riley had a .45 holstered on his right side and shoved a .44 Henry rifle into his saddle boot. The two mounted, gave a wave to Lester, who stood nearby.

Jig Riley led the way by walking his horse to the edge of town then gigged the mount to a trot. Jeremiah maneuvered his horse to ride alongside Jig's horse.

About a mile outside town, Jig pointed to the left at a scattering of buildings, 'That's Charlie Haskel's place. That man has himself a fine-looking wife, French, I think. They got a passel of kids.'

A mile further along, Jig pointed out another farm in the distance. 'That would be the widow Larsen's place. Old Mason, her husband, died a year or so ago, but she will not leave. Got no place to go, I guess.'

They rode in silence for a time then Jig said, 'Might as well give these horses a workout,' as he nudged a spur to his horse's flank. The horse responded immediately stretching out to a full run. Jeremiah followed suit and was able to keep pace. He followed behind for approximately ten minutes until Jig slowed his horse down to a walk. Jeremiah came alongside. 'Does 'em good to work up a sweat,' Jig explained.

After two hours of steady riding, Jig pointed to his left, 'Broken Wagon is over that way. If we had taken that road, we would ride right into the front yard. Straight ahead a couple miles, is Emil Croft's place. Let's ride until we can see the outline of the buildings, then I'll use my telescope to see if anyone's around. We don't want anyone to see us coming in, just yet.'

Ten minutes later, Jig held up a hand. They both could see the roof of a house in the distance. Jig reached back to a saddlebag and took out a surplus Army telescope. He placed the scope to his eye. He fell silent as he studied the yard, barn and house for two or three minutes. 'There's a horse in a corral next to the barn. The barn door is closed and I do not see any activity outside of the house or barn. I think we should ride in slow and see who pokes their head out the door. Be on the lookout, might be a gun barrel that does the talking.'

Jig led the way, both he and Jeremiah kept their reins in their left hand, which left their right hand free and near their six-gun handles. Both men took the keeper thong off the hammers, just in case.

The house and the barn were straight wooden structures and appeared well maintained. The surrounding grounds around both buildings were free of weeds. Someone had gone to a lot of labor to ensure that the place appeared well kept. Jeremiah and Jig were skeptical that the miscreant Emil Croft would put out the effort to keep things this neat and clean.

The two men walked their horses into the yard then stopped twenty feet from the front of the house. The front door opened and a thin man stepped out. He had a double-barreled shotgun in one hand, but did not raise it.

'Howdy,' Jig called out. 'Rest easy, friend, we mean no harm. We're on our way over to Broken Wagon, but these horses could stand a blow and a little water, if you can spare it.'

The man nodded then pointed the muzzle of the shotgun to a trough in front of the corral. 'Help yourself.'

Jig and Jeremiah walked their horses to the trough then dismounted. The thirsty animals began to sup the water immediately. The man from the house stepped nearby, but not real close.

'Did you fellas ride far?'

Jig wagged his head, 'No, actually I live in Stockton, but Jeremiah here is new to the territory. Nicely kept place, you got here. The last time I saw it, it wasn't anywhere near as presentable as it is now.'

'It did take a little doing to get things the way I like them,' the man said.

Jig grinned, 'Well, it sure looks good. Fella named Emil Croft used to own this place. Have you seen him lately?'

The man had a solemn look on his face, 'I moved in some two years ago. I have not seen him since. The name is Otto Randal.'

He looked pale, indicating that he may have some malady or spent most of his time inside a building. He did not look the part of a gambler, but perhaps there were other ways for some to learn the art of swindle rather than toil for their daily dollars.

Jig nodded then stuck out his hand, 'Jig Riley and this is Jeremiah Hackett.' Jeremiah studied the man's face when they shook hands. He was sure that this man's actual name was Otis Rhodes, the thief and supposed fellow escapee, perhaps comrade, to Atwood and Childers. At least, his face and physical being matched the wanted poster he had back in the carriage. That would be something to look into later but not right now. If he were to take the man prisoner, it could hamper his search for Croft.

137

Otto Randal seemed uneasy with the men's presence and said nothing further.

When the horses raised their muzzles from the trough, Jig mounted his horse, as did Jeremiah.

Jig nodded, 'Thanks for the water, Otto. We need to be on our way.'

They trotted their horses out of the yard. When out of sight of the buildings, Jeremiah drew to a halt, as did Jig Riley.

'I figure that he's hiding something. No reason to close up a barn unless you don't want anyone seeing what's in it,' Jig Riley said. 'And Otto was a little too quiet and not very friendly, like damn near anyone else would be if you rode into their yard.'

'I believe that his real name is Otis Rhodes, wanted for escaping prison with Atwood and Childers. If it is Rhodes, there is a five-hundred-dollar reward offered for his capture.'

Jig glared at him, 'You want to take him in for the reward?'

Jeremiah shook his head, 'We could do that later on, but I want to find Croft first. I would not mind seeing the insides of that house and barn. I do not believe that Otto or Otis or whatever he claims his name is, lives there alone. He said that he has been there for two years, but never said if he bought the place. Maybe Croft or some others live there or at least sleep there as well. I would not hold stock to anything the man said. Did you notice that the corral has a lot of not so old horse droppings scattered on the ground? It looks to me that there is way too much for that lone horse to have done.'

CHAPTER 19

By the time they rode to within 500 yards of the trading post, it was late afternoon. The sun hovered just above the western horizon on its way to dip out of sight. Jig flared a hand to an old rusting broken-down wagon with the front wheels missing. 'That's what gives the place its name.'

The trading post was a ramshackle-looking wood-sided building, which had never seen a paintbrush – or any maintenance for that matter. Weeds a foot tall grew close to the sides of the building and concealed what looked to be various rusty broken tools or parts. A covered porch fronting the building had a saggy roof and the board deck under the roof was unleveled and slanting to one side. Barrels holding various used tools sat on either side of the door opening.

Two freight wagons with tarped loads were sitting alongside the building, their four mule teams lazing in their rigging while awaiting the return of their owners. Four horses stood before a hitch rail fronting the trading post. Jig stopped his horse as if in thought of the last time he was here when there had also been four horses, and all hell broke loose.

He gigged his horse to step beside the tied horses. Jeremiah followed suit. They tied their reins then stepped

139

toward an open doorway. Jig entered first with a hand near his six-gun. Jeremiah was one step behind him. They both stepped inside then paused to let their eyes adjust to the dim surroundings. Two scruffy-looking men seated at a table to the left looked their way for only a moment, then back toward the table. Before them sat plates heaped with brown beans and mashed potatoes. A half cake of corn-bread lay on a cloth in the middle of the table. The two men were busy shoveling the simple meal into their mouths.

Four men stood before the bar, two of which by their attire, floppy hats, overalls and brogan shoes, were obvi-ously the freight wagon drivers. Two other men stood to their right nearest to the door. One man was stocky and dark, with a three-day stubble of coarse whiskers on his face; the other was slim, very thin at the waist, almost gaunt in appearance, and he had long, tapering, almost womanish fingers.

Gunslinger hands, Jeremiah thought, smooth and quick and without callouses from any regular use by wage work. Both wore their holsters low down on their thighs, the tips tied down with a thong that encircled the leg just above the knee. Both men turned their heads to glare at the new arrivals.

Ogden McGinty, a short balding man with a big belly stood behind the bar. He held a dingy rag in one hand while wiping a glass in an attempt to clean it. He looked to the door when Jig and Jeremiah entered then spoke, 'Welcome to Broken Wagon, gents. Step right in. I most likely got what you are looking for. If you want something to drink, I have some fresh beer and some old whiskey.'

One of the men having their meal called out, 'Yeah, that old whiskey is at least a week old.'

McGinty was quick to answer with disdain. 'You don't

140

have to drink it, Jubal.'

Jubal grinned, 'Don't take offence, Ogden. I was just saying.'

McGinty turned his attention back to the new arrivals, 'Don't pay the riff-raff any mind, gentlemen. Their only real complaint is that I expect them to pay for what they drink. Now, where was I? Oh yeah, we got plenty of food. Elsie just cooked it up this morning. If you need goods from the store, just look around and let me know. There's water for your animals,' he paused. 'No charge. If'n you need grain for 'em, just see Mort out at the stable and he'll fix you up for a small fee.'

McGinty was still talking when Jig and Jeremiah stepped forward.

When recognition of Jig came to McGinty, he stopped his spiel of offerings abruptly. 'Howdy, Jig. It's been a spell since you were out this way.'

Jig nodded, 'It has at that.'

McGinty eyed him suspiciously, 'I hope you come for a different reason, this time.'

'We're not part of a posse, if that's what you mean,' Jig replied. 'I'm just showing my friend Jeremiah around the country. He's from St Louis, out to see if there is any property for sale that he might invest in.'

McGinty cast a glance to Jeremiah. 'That so,' he said flatly then looked back to Jig.

'It looks like your business is doing well, Ogden,' Jig commented.

McGinty bobbed his head. 'It is increasing. Travelers and freight drivers are less afraid of traveling the roads again ever since they heard the news about how someone killed Lenny Childers and Ben Atwood. Those two sure did cause a lot of problems, but from what I've heard, there's others taking up the slack.'

141

Whether he cared or not, he did not ask how Jig's business was doing.

'You want a drink or something?' McGinty asked.

'Beer,' Jig said. 'We'll take our drinks over to that table.' He pointed to a table sitting behind the two freight drivers.

Jeremiah bobbed his head, 'Beer for me too.'

They stepped to the table while keeping the two gunmen at the bar in their peripheral vision, then sat down. Jeremiah had noticed that the pair had stiffened, their eyes darting to him and Jig when Jig mentioned the word posse to McGinty.

McGinty took two tall mugs from a board shelf behind him then filled them. He brought the mugs to the table and set them down. 'It's a fair brew, made with sorghum and hops and it's only ten cents a mug.'

Jig dropped a quarter onto the tabletop. 'Have you seen Emil Croft lately, Ogden? We were wondering if his place might be for sale.'

Ogden gave Jig a wily look then shook his head. 'Not lately. As far as I know, he left a couple years ago. Fella named Otto something or another lives out to Croft's old place now. What few times I have seen him, he seems to be a quiet sort and keeps to his self. He comes in once and a while to trade some tools and such, buys his supplies, has a few beers then leaves. You might ride over and ask him?'

McGinty scooped up the coin then stepped back behind the bar. One of the two gunmen pulled a turnip watch from his pocket and looked at it then nudged his partner as if they had an appointment somewhere. They downed the last of their whiskey drinks in throwback gulps then set their glasses on the bar. The skinny one cast a glance to Jeremiah and Jig's table, and then the two men left.

142

Jeremiah and Jig drank their beer then they also left. It was now dark outside but a quarter moon's glare gave off enough light for the men to ride without hazard. They rode their horses away from the trading post on the road towards Stockton. After a mile of traveling, Jig pulled his horse to a halt. 'I know Ogden well enough to figure that he's lying. I'd say that he has seen Croft recently, but does not want anyone to know it for some reason. Maybe he is friends with Croft and knows about his rift with me. In addition, I get the feeling that those two gun-slicks at the bar most likely work for Ogden in some unsavory manner. We could follow them and see where they are going. I'm guessing that would most likely be right back to Croft's place.'

Jeremiah thought for a moment. 'You've drawn the same conclusion that I have. I think I would like to ride back to Croft's and see. Who knows, maybe Emil might show up too.'

Jig nodded. 'We can do that, but it might get a bit tricky if they were to see us, then we'd have to find an excuse for stalking the place when it's dark out. I know you want to take down Emil Croft, but going up against those two gunmen might get us both shot.'

'Then let's do our watching from a distance,' Jeremiah said. They rode to the little hillock from where they had first sighted the buildings earlier in the day. Jig figured it was as good as they could get because the corral, barn and house were visible. He extracted the telescope again and brought it to his eye. Jig studied for a moment then brought the scope down, he then turned to face Jeremiah.

Jeremiah took a deep breath, 'What do you think we should do, Jig?'

'Well, I would say we do what we are doing,' Jig said. 'Do our watching, wait, and see what develops. It appears to me, that something does not seem to fit. It just doesn't look right. The buildings and surrounding yard are too clean, for one thing, as if he is trying to hide something. I would wager that if we wait long enough, someone is going to come along and we will find out what is going on. Let's loosen the cinches on our horses, let 'em graze while we do our looking. We might as well have something to eat while we're at it.'

Both men stepped to their horses and loosened the saddles, then took the bits from the horses' mouths but left the bridles on with the reins trailing to the ground. Being ground-tied, the horses would not wander far. Jig rummaged into his saddlebags and brought out a few strips of jerky, handing some to Jeremiah. The two munched on the jerky, washing it down with canteen water.

When they had finished eating, Jeremiah offered, 'I'll take the first watch, if you want to rest a bit, Jig.'

Jig bobbed his head then got a bedroll from behind his saddle, rolled it out and lay down. About midnight Jeremiah nudged the sleeping man's boot.

'Nothing yet,' Jeremiah said when Jig sat up.

About four o'clock, Jig shook Jeremiah's shoulder. Jeremiah blinked awake. Jig held a palm down in the moonlight indicating that he should be quiet.

'A wagon and two outriders just pulled up to the barn,' Jig said, then handed the telescope to Jeremiah.

Jeremiah closed one eye while staring through the telescope with the other.

'Looks like a fully-loaded freight wagon. A saddle horse is trailing behind the wagon. One of the riders just opened the barn door and the wagon is being driven in,' Jeremiah declared. 'They are too far away for me to tell who was driving the wagon and who the rider is.'

In a short time, the four-mule wagon team and the riders' horses were shooed into the coral and the barn door closed shut. The three men then began walking toward the house where, since their arrival, lamplight had appeared in the windows.

'We're going to need to get a look in the windows to see if we can learn something,' Jig said.

'Do we walk from here?' Jeremiah asked.

Jig shook his head. 'Let's take the horses and ride around real quiet like to the back of that barn. Then we can sneak over to the house and look in the window. I have a hunch that those two we saw at McGinty's place have something to do with this. Could be that wagon belonged to one of those freighters we saw in the trading post and has fallen into a thieves' lair. If that is so, then those two were just following him along then met up with someone else, possibly a lookout, and then they set their trap. When ready, they jumped the freighter and took his goods. I sure hope they didn't kill that poor fella.'

Five minutes later Jig mounted his horse then led the way with Jeremiah following close behind. The men walked their horses in a circular route to come up behind the barn. They ground tied their horses behind the barn. Each man pulled his six-gun and checked the loads. Jeremiah then took his shotgun from the saddle rig while Jig pulled his rifle out of the scabbard.

They worked their way alongside the barn then crouched to hurry across the yard to the house. Thank God, there was no dog around to sound an alarm. Both men stayed low and made their way to a window that was spilling light outside. Someone had lifted the window up in its frame, a few inches for ventilation. By standing in a crouch position to one side, Jig could look in the window

145

without the room occupants' knowledge. The two men they had seen at McGinty's were sprawled on a stuffed couch facing the door. To their left a man sat in a ladder-back chair while the fourth, Otto Randal stood in the middle of the room. He was talking to the others.

'Well, you men only did half of what you were supposed to do. We need both of those wagons. The cargo is too valuable to pass up.'

Jig dropped down and touched Jeremiah's arm so that he could get a look. Jeremiah moved into position and stared in. His eyes widened in recognition of the man in the ladder-back chair. Emil Croft!

Jeremiah stiffened and began to bring his shotgun up. Jig reached over and grabbed hold of Jeremiah's shoulder. He grimaced while shaking his head. Jeremiah moved to crouch below the window. Jig held up a hand to put a finger to his lips, indicating for Jeremiah to be quiet and still. Jig wanted to hear the rest of what the robbers had to say.

One of the gunmen spoke up, 'We did what we could, Otis. We caught up to the one driver making a camp out by Dry Creek. We waited a couple hours for the other one to show up but he never did.'

The other gunman on the couch decided to explain, 'The driver said the other one got into the bottle and decided to spend some time with that whore McGinty keeps. He told his partner that he'd be along in the morning.'

'It ain't likely that those two freighters would split up. How's come the one you got decided to go on alone?' Otto asked disdainfully.

'He said that he didn't want to have to pay McGinty's price for boarding his mules. They could just as well feed free out on the prairie. That's what he said before Emil snuffed his wick.'

Otto turned his head to face Emil Croft. 'You killed him?'

Croft nodded, 'Yeah, I did. I would have left him bound until he started in begging. Said we could have everything, he just wanted us to leave him unharmed. I never could stand a man to go sniveling. It reminded me of my youngest boy, always whining, so I sliced his throat. Nobody is likely to find him. I drug his carcass into a thicket.'

Otis stood stiff-legged. 'Robbing is one thing, but killing travelers will cause the law to come nosing around, which none of us want to happen.'

'Couldn't be helped,' Croft cut in. 'That fella was cat-erwauling something fierce. I had to shut him up.'

Otto glared at Croft with disapproval. After a moment, he turned to face the gunmen. 'Well, what's done is done, I guess, but you all can't lounge around while there's still work to do. You have to get back on the road and get that other wagon before he gets away. There is no need to kill him. Just bind him up good so that we can get the wagons out of the country before someone figures that they are missing.'

'Hell, we've been up all night, Otis,' one of the gunmen complained. 'We need to rest up a bit; a few hours ain't going to mean anything. We'll catch up to him. We might just as well let him handle that team as long as we can. He is headed our way, anyway.'

CHAPTER 20

Jig grabbed a hold of Jeremiah's arm, pulled him away from the window, and headed toward the barn. He held onto Jeremiah's arm until they got back to their horses.

Once there, Jeremiah shook his arm free. 'What the hell, Jig, you heard them. That's Emil Croft in there and he admitted to murdering that freighter. Why don't we knock down that nest of vipers while we got the opportunity?'

Jig held a hand up, 'Hold on there, Jeremiah, we'll get to taking them down in due time. I have been doing some thinking. Before we open the dance, let's do a little cogitating. Now, I do not care if you kill Croft for what he has done past and present, but to my knowledge there is no paper on him. It might be a stretch to explain things to Grosser if we kill them all without him arresting us both for murder. I've already told you that Grosser will only see things through the eyes of the law and we need to show him the whole show.'

Jeremiah jerked his head to stare at Jig. 'It is my intent to see that Emil Croft pays for his crime, in like manner to what he did to George Finimin.'

Jig bobbed his head. 'I understand your feelings on the matter. I have like feelings for those that killed Marshal

Hames. For all I know, those two gunnies sitting in the house might be the guilty ones. What I do know is that it would not be a smart thing for you to either get yourself hanged or spend the rest of your life in prison for killing the likes of Emil Croft. There's a better way to make him pay a dearer price without sacrificing yourself in the doing.'

Jig paused for a moment then continued, 'We both heard him admit to killing that freighter, so if we took him in alive we can testify that we both heard him say what he did. I would wager that the judge will sentence Emil Croft to hang. It gets to be pretty hard on a man's mind, quite torturous in fact, if he knows that he is going to hang and cannot do anything but wait. He will count off the days then the hours and then the minutes until that they come for him. It seems to me that it would be better for you to know that Croft is suffering, rather than for you having to explain why you killed him. The way I figure it, if you got arrested, the whole story would sooner or later be laid bare and the judge might frown on knowing you were hunting Croft down to kill him.'

Jig paused for a moment, and then said, 'I know you got it into your head to handle this on your own, but I'd sure hate to see you end up on the wrong side of the law. You think about it for a few minutes. We have an opportunity to take down a whole gang and maybe find out who's the ringleader if we don't kill all of them.'

He paused again, and then said, 'It's up to you, Jeremiah, and I'll do whatever you think is right. When you are ready, we will go and get them. I have no problem shooting those two gunmen, but we need to take Croft and that fella Otto in alive, if we can. Once behind bars, I can guarantee that one of them will do about anything in order to hold off the hangman and save his own skin. He is bound to talk and maybe that will lead to who's on the other end receiving the stolen goods.'

Jeremiah had quietly listened to Jig intently, understanding everything the man said. He felt he could trust the man and what Jig had said made sense. He was so intent on revenge that he had not thought of having to pay a price for killing Croft. Hell, the son-of-a-bitch deserved to die for what he had done and Jeremiah had prepared himself to do the shooting. Now the opportunity was here and he did not want that opportunity to escape.

Jeremiah thought of everything that had happened since the night that George had died.

Things were a little different now, he knew that he had changed and had matured. He had learned to be patient when the circumstance demanded it. Then later, he had acquired the skills required to be deadly when forced. Though circumstance had him there, he had come to like his current way of living. Jeremiah was glad that he agreed to be Lester's guardian. He enjoyed working at Lester's place and their trips to town and getting to know Lucy Meadows. He wanted to become more involved with her; perhaps he would offer to buy a half share of the farm from Lester to cement things. Surely he and Lester could figure out a way to make a living, perhaps raise some cattle or sell some potions into new territory and use the farm as home base.

Jeremiah took a breath then nodded, 'Okay, we'll do it your way, Jig. I am ready. I will only shoot Croft to put him down so's he cannot escape. I'll do the same to Otis if he tries anything while you work on those two gunmen.'

Jig nodded, 'Let's go do it then. We do not have much time; it is going to get light before long. You take the window. I'll take the door. Soon as I open that door, get ready for some shooting.'

Jig and Jeremiah crept alongside the barn then peered around to make sure no one was watching from the house. When they figured it was clear, they retraced their earlier steps back to the window. Jig leaned his rifle against the building then drew his six-gun with his right hand. Jeremiah had already cocked both hammers of the shotgun before they had begun to come back to the house.

First Jig looked in the window, then Jeremiah. The men inside were still in the same positions that they had been in when Jig and Jeremiah had first looked in. The two gunmen were on the couch and Emil Croft was still sitting in the wooden chair. Otis was standing to the right of the gunmen with a cup of coffee in his hand.

Jig, with six-gun held at waist level, stepped over to the steps of the porch. He tiptoed up the three steps onto the porch then advanced to stand in front of the door. He reached his left hand to grasp the doorknob then he looked over to Jeremiah and nodded. Jeremiah brought the shotgun up and smashed it through the window glass as Jig opened the door and stepped inside. The breaking of the glass, as well as a man with a gun in hand barging in the front door, startled the men inside. Both men on the couch immediately reached for their six-guns while jumping to their feet. The only thing that saved Jig was that both men had keeper thongs on their six-gun hammers and had to flick them off before they could draw.

Jig hollered out, 'Don't move or I'll shoot!'

Both men ignored the warning. When Jig saw what they were doing, he opened fire. The taller of the two men took two slugs to his chest, which flung him back to land on the couch. The man triggered his six-gun in his death throe but the bullet went harmlessly into the floor two feet in front of Jig.

The other gunman, the stocky one, managed to get his six-gun out of his holster and was attempting to raise it up when Jig's six-gun barked twice more. The man took one slug in his stomach and the other one just where the throat met the chest. A spray of blood and bone chips painted the couch behind him. He fell backwards by the impacts of the bullets but managed to trigger his six-gun in his death drop.

Jeremiah had timed it to stick the muzzle of the shotgun through the window as soon as Jig pushed open the front door. He had the muzzle lined up on Emil Croft. Emil had jumped to his feet as well and was drawing his six-gun as Jig began shooting the others. Jeremiah desperately wanted to pull the trigger while the shotgun aimed at Croft's torso but lowered the muzzle down a bit and tripped one of the triggers. The result was that some of the buckshot turned the chair legs into pieces of kindling while the rest of the buckshot ripped through Emil Croft's lower legs. The blast knocked Croft off his feet. The man flung his six-gun aside as he grabbed his legs with both hands then curled to hold his now bloody mangled legs and began to scream mournfully.

Jeremiah turned the shotgun toward Otis, who was standing in the gunsmoke-filled room with his mouth open and face as pale as a newly-washed sheet. It appeared that Otis was unarmed and was not going to take part in the shooting as he dropped the coffee cup and raised his arms in submission. Jeremiah glanced away to see if he should trip that other trigger into the gunmen before the couch. At that time, Jig had just fired the two rounds into the second gunman and that man's six-gun fired. The bullet, though errant, caught Jeremiah in his upper left shoulder. It was enough to propel him backwards to land on his butt.

Jeremiah was stunned but managed to sit up just as the door opened and Otis stepped out with his hands raised. Jig followed with six-gun in hand. Seeing that Jeremiah was down, Jig wasted no time in voicing his concern. 'Damn, Jeremiah, have you been hit?'

He took a hand to push Otis a step past Jeremiah, 'Don't make any move fella while I see to my partner.'

Jig held his six-gun so that he could still use it should Otis try anything while he kneeled down. With his other hand, he opened Jeremiah's jacket and shirtfront then he checked Jeremiah's back but found no exit wound.

'I don't think it hit a bone, but that bullet's still in there, Jeremiah. We need to get you to a doctor right away. That fella Croft is in need of some patching as well.'

He stood then said to Otis, 'Need you to do what you can to clean up this wound on Jeremiah and then see what you can do to keep Croft from bleeding out. You do what I say, I'll mention it to the judge.'

Otis nodded.

'Is there a buckboard or some wheeled vehicle inside that barn we can use to get these men to a doctor?' Jig asked.

Otis nodded again. 'There's a buckboard inside the barn on the left. The rigging is hanging on the wall.'

Jig then turned to Jeremiah. 'You think you can go inside, sit down and watch over Otis while he tends to you and Croft? I'll hitch up a wagon, so's we can be on our way.'

Jeremiah nodded then said through gritted teeth, 'Yeah, I can do that, Jig. I have my six-gun ready and I still got one barrel of this shotgun ready to use.'

153

It was less than half an hour later that Jig had the buck-board parked out front of the house. He and Otis lugged the bodies of the two gunmen out and loaded them into the wagon. Then Jig and Otis lugged the whining Emil Croft to lie alongside the two bodies. Jeremiah took a seat to lean against a side rail inside the wagon box right behind the seat. He could keep an eye on the driver, which would be Otis, while Jig rode alongside. He had tied Jeremiah's horse to the back of the wagon.

It was mid-morning when the wagon rolled to a stop in front of the jailhouse. Jig pulled his horse to a hitch rail fronting the jail just as Emmett Grosser stepped out with a look of wonder on his face.

Jig and Grosser exchanged a few words then Grosser called out to watchful George Dill, the barber, to fetch Doctor Cudahy. Jig helped Jeremiah down while Grosser and Otis carried Emil Croft into a jail cell and lay him on a bunk. Grosser then herded Otis into an adjoining cell and locked the cell door.

Within ten minutes, Doctor Cudahy had looked at Jeremiah's wound and said, 'Need to get you over to my office. I will have to dig for that bullet. George will help you over there and Nurse Ritter will see to you until I can get there. Right now, that other fella is in worse shape than you are. He has lost a lot of blood. I have to get him bound up before he loses anymore. It does not look good. We may lose him.'

Three weeks later, despite Doctor Cudahy's early assess-ment, Emil Croft lay on his bunk in the jail and he was very much alive and complaining.

'Hey, Emmett, when is that judge due to show up here? I still say it is a waste of time going to court. Nobody can prove anything against me, specially saying that I killed some freight driver. I mean, hell, they ain't no witnesses. Jig and that other fella come out to my place shooting without any cause. They killed Shade and Bascom. Shot 'em down like they was dogs, then they like to killed me. I don't even know who that young one is. I never saw him before. You ought to, at least, let Otis go on back out to my place. Hell, Otis is just my caretaker and he don't know nothing.'

'Save it for the judge, Croft.' Grosser replied.

EPILOGUE

Jeremiah had healed reasonably well after three weeks of either lying around in the hotel room or visiting Jig and Lester down at the livery. Doctor Cudahy had used chloroform to put him out while he dug out the .45 slug that was deep in his shoulder muscle. He felt pretty good right now and hoped that he never again would feel the impact of a bullet. At the doctor's insistence, he kept his arm in a sling. He would argue that point on his next visit to the doctor. Jeremiah was getting anxious for him and Lester to head back to Hays City as soon as Croft's trial was over. Actually, he would stay long enough to see that Croft hanged, no matter how long it took.

Jeremiah and Jig Riley had split up the bounties paid out on the wanted men that they had brought in. Otis Rhodes was worth five hundred dollars. Both Leonard Bascom and Wilber Shade were worth a thousand dollars each. The men, wanted for at least two murders each in both Arkansas and Texas and numerous robberies in Kansas, were a bounty hunter's prize.

Two days later a trial held for Otis Rhodes and Emil Croft began.

Rhodes had earlier admitted his involvement in seeing to the disposal of stolen merchandise and named those involved who were receiving it on the other end. Judge Larsen had already issued orders to Colorado officers to pick up the other individuals named. During testimony, it appeared that Rhodes really did not involve himself in the actual robberies. He was just the stolen merchandise disposal man. He admitted that he had escaped prison along with Lenny Childers and Ben Atwood. The three had cooked up the scheme then carried it forward. Rhodes did not have much to say about Ogden McGinty, other than that he was a hard man to deal with. At no time did he say that McGinty was involved in the scheme.

Sheriff McDaniel back in Hays City had everything figured out as far as where the merchandise ended up. The only thing he erred in was that he believed that George McGinty was involved in handling stolen merchandise. As it turned out thought, McGinty had no connection to the scheme. McGinty did not need to. He was making a good living just as things were.

However, just two miles away, Otis Rhodes had buddied up with Emil Croft. Croft was the one who had induced Bascom and Shade to fill the gap soon after the news of Atwood and Childers' demise. Croft remained aloof, preferring to spend his time in solo stealing while Rhodes acted as a front.

The trial lasted two days while witnesses as well as the accused gave testimony.

Rhodes, being an escaped prisoner, was worried about his fate. He knew he could go back to prison, but he also knew that the judge could just as easily send him to the gallows.

Judge Larsen ordered Rhodes and Croft to stand before him. Rhodes stood straight while Croft sat in a wheel chair.

'Otis Rhodes, you have been convicted of breaking out

of prison, then associating with some vile miscreants. You put yourself on the road to ruin and assisted others in numerous robberies. Though you did not participate in the killing of innocent travelers, your supporting those that did those awful crimes makes you an accessory to those crimes. In other words, you are just as guilty as the actual killers.'

Rhodes sucked in his wind as the judge paused for a moment.

Judge Larsen cleared his throat. 'The court recognizes the guilty pleas you have made and your assistance in naming those who are just as guilty. In that light, the court feels merciful and therefore sentences you to life in prison without parole.'

The judge then turned his attention to the man in the wheelchair.

'Emil Croft, you have been accused of numerous acts of chicanery, that span a number of years. Unfortunately, until now, you have not had to answer for any of those crimes. Today, however, a jury who believes that you murdered one Mordechai Johansen at his campsite convicted you. You then hid his body and stole all his possessions, claiming them as your own. You then confessed that fact to your cohorts, which included Otis Rhodes. Fortunately, witnesses Jig Riley and Jeremiah Hackett were just outside your window and able to hear your confession as well.'

'They got no body, Judge,' Croft cut in. 'No proof.'

Judge Larsen smiled lightly, 'Oh, but you are wrong, Mr Croft. A search team found the remains of Mister Johansen. Apparently, no one saw the need to inform you. Doctor Cudahy wrote out his autopsy findings. It is quite gruesome. The man's throat had been sliced ear to ear just as you had said you had done.

'It is the judgement of this court that you be hanged by

the neck until you are dead. The sentence is to be carried out within seventy-two hours.'

The judge tapped his gavel then turned and left.

On the day of Emil Croft's scheduled hanging, Jeremiah parked his emblazoned carriage in front of the jail, in plain view for all to see. Jeremiah had not spoken one word to Emil Croft before or during the trial, but he wanted to be sure that Croft, on his way to the gallows, saw the carriage.

Immediately after the hanging, Jeremiah and Lester said their goodbyes to Jig Riley then left town. While on the road, Jeremiah struck a deal with Lester agreeing to sell half his share of the farm to Jeremiah.

Six months later, out at the farm, Jeremiah and Lester had bought half a dozen white-faced shorthorn yearling cattle with the intent to see if they could raise them profitably. Jeremiah parked the sales carriage and put Chelsea out to pasture. There had been no potion sales since Lester had sold a few bottles back in Stockton. Jeremiah had no immediate plans to revive the business. After a meeting with Sheriff McDaniel, Jeremiah agreed to become a deputy sheriff. He and Lucy Meadows had made plans to marry in the spring.